Tales of Junction

Tales of Junction

Guy Cain
and
John L. Davis IV

Dedications

John – For my family, as always.

Guy - For my part, I'd like to thank my mother, Marilyn Tomlinson, for always being supportive no matter how crazy my ideas seemed.

Table of Contents

John L. Davis IV – Guy Cain

Lost in the Wilderness

Frito was getting hungry. Real hungry. He'd been out for fifteen days and, at this point, he was beginning to dream longingly of Filler's stew. He'd brought some with him as usual, but it had run out around day five. For what seemed like the hundredth time, he checked the pockets of his camo jacket in hopes of finding one last bag of corn chips but came up empty. Nothing left to do but keep moving. As best as he could figure, there was a river a day's walk to the south. Once he got there he could set up a few lines and maybe get a couple fish.

Rarely did the life of a scav get this bad. Most of the time, on these long runs, he'd come across something edible while scavenging, but this run had been a complete bust. Everywhere he went had been picked clean by someone else. The remote farm houses that usually provided a couple jars of canned vegetables were all occupied by small tribes of foul-smelling Sores.

He wondered if tribe was the correct word to describe them. Maybe herd would be more appropriate given that they weren't human in the eyes of most people. Genetically they were; but, to be honest, they lived like animals, acted like animals and hunted like animals. No matter how you chose to describe them, they were best avoided. Especially by a lone scav.

He hadn't planned to be out this long but it all went awry when he crossed paths with a band of gypsies. These bastards were better organized than most and reasonably well equipped. They had at least four vehicles and easily thirty well-armed men. He'd smelled their fire well in advance and was trying to skirt around the encampment when he was spotted by one of their sentries.

These guys weren't messing around. They had tracked Frito for days. Every time he stopped to rest, they would catch up. In the end he had kept moving. No stopping to rest or sleep, moving constantly, leading them further away from Junction until he was finally able to circle around them and start towards home.

Now, it was just a matter of avoiding the Sores, zombies, dehydration and starvation. Pretty much a normal day in the life of a scav. Still, he was going to need to eat something soon. Hunger lead to poor judgement and poor judgement would get a man killed in this world. Furthermore, if he returned to Junction with nothing to show from this trip, Filler would be unbearable. A couple of dry runs and the fat bastard might cut off even the best scavenger.

He could see a stormfront moving in from the west. It was going to be an uncomfortable night if he didn't find some shelter soon. He kept walking knowing that at the very least he was getting closer to Junction and the gypsies were most likely moving further away. As the first drops of rain began to fall he noticed a mail box along the road in the distance. He looked around hoping to find a deserted farm house but could only see a few trees at the end of a driveway. With no other options and the storm nearly upon him, he made for the trees.

2

The trees had hidden the burned remains of a home and barn. The basement of the house was nearly full of stagnant water. Pieces of the tin roof of the old barn remained propped up by a rusted tractor skeleton, it's tires melted away during the fire. Frito figured it would make a passable shelter for the night, and that's when he noticed the mound of earth. As the rain began to pour down, he pulled on the weathered door of the root cellar, revealing shelves lined with Mason jars.

The next morning, both his stomach and duffel bag were full. It was rare to get this lucky, but when it happened it was glorious. The jars were heavy but would lighten up as he traveled. Frito figured to eat his fill on the way back to Junction. The up side to being a scav was that you got first choice of everything you found, provided Filler didn't find out.

Friends

Frito and Tool made plans to go scavenging together a few times a year. On a couple occasions, Filler let them rent the old VW Beetle so they could cover some distance. The rent usually amounted to half of their haul, but they didn't mind. These runs weren't just about scavenging. It was a chance for the friends to get away from the smell of hogs and unwashed humans, the smells of Junction.

The VW Beetle was Filler's pride and joy. He had converted it to run on alcohol after his truck was trashed during his last scavenging run with Bill Robb ages ago. The conversion wasn't even that difficult. In high school Filler had converted a motor in his automotive class but had never been allowed to test it because the school frowned on distilling alcohol even for the purposes of fuel. Filler knew that the air-cooled motor of the old VW was a perfect candidate and the previous owner was more than happy to part with it, as gas was no longer available.

Each time they ventured out together, Filler would give them a "wish list." This time was no exception.

"When are you taking off?"

"You know Tool, he wants to leave at night, but if we're taking the Beetle, I figure we should wait until day-break."

"Ok Frito, I'll have the Beetle ready. Extra fuel and some food under the hood, but I need for you guys to find a few things for me."

Frito smiled, "I'd expect no less. Do you have a list?"

"Still working on it. I'll leave it on the driver's seat. You'll be responsible for it, since your buddy doesn't know how to read."

"Easy, Filler. You can't talk like that about my boy. Tool's a good scav and he's had my back more times than I can count."

"Whatever you say, but as far as I'm concerned, this is your run, not his. Don't let anything happen to my wheels. Filler started to walk away then turned to add, "First on that list is tires for the bug. There's rope in the car, get as many as you can and tie them to the doors if that's what it takes."

"Sure thing Filler." Frito was laughing inside. Filler hadn't been outside the walls in years. He had no idea what it was like. Everything from the old world had value to the citizens of Junction. The problem was that very little remained of that world. There was a reason that the "bowls" they served food in were actually old hub caps. The zombies staggered through the world without regard for anything. The Sores were even worse, smashing anything that would break to make their primitive weapons and traps. Entire towns have been burned to the ground, leaving nothing but ashes and brick shells. Finding tires to fit the Beetle was no small order, but Frito and Tool were the best scavs that Junction had to offer. If anyone could find some, it was them.

Frito was going through his gear one last time when he heard footsteps outside his shack. There was a light rapping on the makeshift door followed by a feminine voice, "Frito, you home?"

"That you, Trina? Come on in."

"Heard you were leaving in the morning. Wanted to wish you luck."

"Thanks, but I'm guessing you are hoping we'll bring something back for you." Frito smiled as he spoke. He liked the part-time teacher, part-time prostitute. It was hard not to like Trina. She treated everyone in Junction to a friendly smile regardless of their standing in the community and it was the kind of smile that made you feel good.

"That obvious, huh?" Frito felt a glow in his chest that spread throughout his body as she feigned embarrassment and flashed him a demur look before producing a short list.

"It's for the school. I can pay you when we have time."

Frito nearly blushed at the thought of being paid by the beautiful school teacher before blurting out, "We'll figure out something."

"Thanks, Frito." Trina suddenly leaned in and gave him a small kiss on the cheek before turning to leave and adding, "I'll be waiting for you."

Trina's words and that little kiss had him so flustered it was several minutes before Frito could finish the task at hand. His gear now checked and double checked, Frito grabbed the pack and headed over to check on Tool. The two scavs were close. They'd hit it off almost immediately. Tool was a self-proclaimed asshole. Frito, the perpetual nice guy. Like yin and yang, the two seemed to feed off one another's energy and became an unstoppable force when they were together.

Tool was just emerging from the short door of his shack as Frito approached.

"Hey, I was just coming to get you. Let's throw our stuff in the bug, grab a bite at Filler's, then head over to Janet's?"

Frito shook his head. "Brother, you are getting a bit predictable, but you left out the part where we get drunk."

"Knew I was forgetting something. Thanks for reminding me."

"Tool, you know we are leaving at dawn, right?"

"Well then, what are we waiting for? Let's get started."

Mitch Burton was just taking his place on the gate wall when he heard the VW sputter to life. Mitch knew the sound and had the night guard stick around long enough to open the gate for the duo. Mitch waved and yelled down to them, "How about you bring back some decent liquor this time?" Tool gave a dismissive wave with his free hand, while the other shaded his bloodshot eyes from the rising sun. Mitch had a laugh at Tool's expense. The scav had over done it the previous night and was now paying the price. Frito had planned on driving the first day as he knew Tool would be in no shape for it and Filler would not be pleased to see Tool behind the wheel of the Bug under any circumstances. Besides, the first day would be nothing more than driving to get as far away from Junction as possible.

Three days into the run and the scavs were feeling great. Only a few withered undead crossed their path and not a single sign of sores. They hadn't found much of value until they stumbled upon a small antique shop in the middle of nowhere with living quarters on the second floor. The place was a gold mine. In no time at all they had made a large pile in the middle of the ground floor, consisting of old files, hand operated drills, three saws, a couple axes, and much more.

"Hey Frito. All this stuff ain't gonna fit in the Bug."

"I was just thinking the same thing. Have you checked out back to see if there's a wagon or something we can pull behind?"

"Yeah. No wagon. No trailer. No car. Not even a garage."

"Well then, you got any ideas?"

"I was thinking we keep piling it up. Spend the night here, then head out tomorrow and see if we can find anything that would work."

"Sounds like a plan to me. I really didn't want to sleep in the car tonight anyway. Let's finish up down here and see what we can find upstairs"

The two scavs were pleased with their haul and jammed wooden chairs in front of the doors before heading to the second floor. The studio type living quarters were extravagant by their standards despite the dust covering everything. They checked the cupboards and found several plastic canisters containing various dry goods, sugar, flour, beans, salt and instant tea. A few cans of food were also present, so they decided to forego their usual meal of brown stew. As the sun set the two friends shared stories over cold green beans and creamed corn.

Morning found them well rested and ready to

get back on the road. They moved the food stuffs down to the ground floor with the other goods before heading out. They had gone only a few miles when they came across a long defunct carnival. The rides were falling apart. The chairs dangling precariously from the Ferris wheel creaked in the light breeze. The large trucks that had brought the rides to their final resting place looked as if they might be washed off and driven away, but for the rotted tires.

The pair brought the old VW to a stop a hundred yards from the carnival, unsure how to proceed.

"Well Frito, it's your call. What do we do?"

"My call? You're behind the wheel. "

"Yeah, but Filler put you in charge of this run, remember?"

"For fuck sake. When have you ever given a shit about anything Filler said?"

Tool feigned a stunned expression for just a moment, then unable to hold it back any longer, both men burst out in laughter. When they finally caught their breath again, "Guess I can't argue that one. Let's sit here for a bit and watch for movement. If we don't see anything we'll circle around and try to draw them out."

"Them? Are you thinking Sores or zombies?"

"Honestly, I think the place is too clean for Sores. We're downwind and could probably smell the stinking things from here. Honestly, man, you gotta wonder how anything living can actually smell worse than zombies. If anything, there's probably just a few huskers bumping around."

"I hope you're right. I'd hate to run into

anything serious in Filler's baby."

"Speaking of his fatness, have we found anything that was on his list?"

"Nothing really. Besides tires, he wants vegetable seeds."

"Seeds? Are you shitting me?"

"Something to do with genetic diversity for the gardens. All I know is that he and Janet said the same thing."

"What about Trina? Have you found anything from her list?" Tool shot a sly grin at his buddy.

"Ya know, I almost asked how you knew, then I remembered, there are no secrets in Junction."

The last words were said in unison by both men.

"Found a couple children's books and a notebook back there. We gotta find a way to get all that stuff back."

"We're the best scavs in Junction, maybe in the whole world. Well, I am anyway." Tool teased his friend.

"Fuck you."

"You're not my type. Besides, Trina would get jealous. Pretty sure she wants you all to herself."

"Let's concentrate on the current problem. We need to figure out a way to get all that stuff back to Junction."

"There must be something in there we can use. A trailer of some sort." Tool nodded towards the rusting carnival. "What say we circle around now? I haven't seen any movement at all."

They slowly made their way around the

abandoned carnival weaving through the saplings that had grown up in the field surrounding it. Once they had reached the entrance without coming under attack by either living or undead, they opted to drive up close and park the beetle.

They carefully picked their way down the midway, making mental notes on locations that may hold items of value, while looking for signs of danger. The carnival looked as if all the patrons and workers had simply vanished. There was no sign that humans had been there in at least a decade. Not even the usual smell of rat feces and urine that Tool and Frito had come to recognize.

"The trailers in the back, behind the games, are going to be our best bet, you think?" Frito whispered just loud enough to be heard by his fellow scav a few feet away.

"Yeah. I had hoped we could just use one of those little food wagons, but the damn tires are rotted off everything. "

"Let's find something and get out of here. This place is creepy as hell." Frito glanced about furtively from rusted rides to the fun house and "Tunnel of Love." He'd seen a lot since the world went to the dead, but this place was the worst. Something about the lack of destruction. Not a single broken window or burned out trailer.

They made their way to a large storage trailer with clowns and laughing children barely discernable on the side. It took a bit of force to get the doors open but Tool managed while Frito kept watch for anything that may be lurking nearby. The trailer was mostly empty, but Tool turned and gave his friend a short whistle and a beckoning nod.

"What did you find?"

"Those!" Tool pointed to four dusty red hand carts all parked in a row against the far wall.

"What the fuck are we gonna do with those? We can't exactly push them back to Junction."

"You're right about that, but I have a plan my dear boy. Take these and follow me."

Frito grabbed the proffered carts as Tool took the remaining two and headed around the front of the trailer.

"There! There's our answer." Tool pointed to a long row of blue, plastic, portable toilets.

"You're joking. You must be joking. "

"We'll leave the hand carts here for now and go get the beetle. Filler sent plenty of rope along for his fucking tires. We lash the carts to a handicap toilet, the larger one on the end, lay it on its side, and POW! We got us a trailer."

"A rolling shit-box! Tool, you're a mad genius. Let's get to it."

Once back at the bug, Frito turned to his partner, "You probably think I'm paranoid, but I think we are being watched."

"You're not paranoid. I saw movement in the window of that camper-trailer. At first I thought it might just be a rat, but it moved away when I looked directly at it."

"Are you fucking with me? Why didn't you say something?"

"Look, we can drive around the outer perimeter, get everything hooked up and be out of here in minutes. Besides, it's probably just some husker. Stick with me, and you'll be back in Trina's arms in no time."

"You just aren't gonna let that go are you."

Tool smiled at his friend's frustration before responding, "Come on, buddy. You know me better than that. When have I ever..." Tool let the sentence trail off as Frito began to laugh loudly.

"Ok, asshole. Just drive the fucking car already."

Working together, it took the scavs about a half hour to lash the two wheeled carts to the port-o-potty and then tie the makeshift trailer to the rear bumper of the bug.

Once out on the road, they found that their trailer pulled reasonably well at low speeds but became unstable if they went much over twenty miles per hour. They hoped that the added weight of the tools and other items would make it pull better for their return trip. Still, both men were quite relieved to watch the dilapidated carnival disappear as they crested the hill on their way back to the antique store.

There was still plenty of daylight when they got back to the antique shop, but they were in no hurry and decided to spend another night in luxury. Like every scav, they had considered finding a place just like this one, far away from people, and just taking it over, making it home. Also, like every other scav, they knew there was safety in a group, and Junction, even though it was a filthy hole, was probably the safest of any place they had seen.

One more thorough search turned up a few

additional items to add to their pile. As the sun began to set the pair wasted little time securing the doors and heading up to the second story to eat and get some rest.

"Hand me that salt. Maybe it will improve Filler's stew. "

"Why do you think I put chips in it. Anything is an improvement." Frito produced a small bag and started crunching them up over the jar of cold stew. "Did you really see something in that camper?"

"Yeah, but it was probably just some solitary sore that knew better than to start shit with a couple bad asses like us. Well, me anyway."

"Tool, you never fail to amuse…" Frito paused before adding, "…yourself."

"You think it might have been something else out there? A twisted maybe?"

Frito looked up from his jar of stew, "The thought had crossed my mind."

"Think about all the times we've been out. Have you ever seen anything other than dead heads or sores?"

"There are more things in heaven and earth, Tool." Tool stared at his friend briefly before shaking his head as Frito continued, "Just because we haven't seen one doesn't mean they aren't out there."

"Look, the twisted are a ghost story. Nothing more. An urban legend like the Jersey Devil or Bigfoot."

"Oh hell no! Don't get me started on Bigfoot." Tool was just about to reply when Frito began to laugh.

"You got me." Tool said, shaking his head

and muttering, "asshole."

The next morning the scavs loaded all their treasures into the port-o-john trailer.

"It doesn't make sense that this place has gone untouched for so many years. Know what I mean?"

"Yeah, somebody should have ransacked it by now. There's definitely something eerie going on. For once I'm actually looking forward to getting back to Junction."

"Speaking of Junction, do we want to pull a few items out before we get there? I mean, Filler is gonna be pretty happy with the haul, even if we didn't find any tires for him, no reason we can't hold back a few things for ourselves."

"Way ahead of you Frito. Got my pack filled with good stuff."

"What about your gear?"

"Put as much as I could in my jacket pockets. Freed up plenty of space. Probably buy me a few nights of company over at Janet's."

"Tool, you are one sneaky sumbitch. I think I'll let you drive the first shift."

The trip back to Junction was taking considerably longer than hoped. Their outhouse trailer wobbled severely as the beetle gained speed. The scavs had gotten into the groove, stopping often to adjust the hand carts and ropes. It was tedious but necessary to keep from scattering their haul across the road should the trailer turn over in transit.

Tool woke to the sound of rain on the roof of

the beetle. The car wasn't moving.

"Can't see the road for the rain?"

"Yeah. Don't want to risk losing our cargo and the wipers aren't working."

"You're a regular comedian. We'll wait here for a bit. Hopefully, it will let up soon."

"Sounds like a plan. I'll go back to sleep then."

Tool rested his head against the window and drifted back to sleep. It seemed he had only just closed his eyes when Frito nudged him awake.

"We got a little problem here."

"Nothing serious I hope."

"She won't start."

"What? Are you fucking with me? Please tell me you're joking."

"Sorry. All it does is click"

"Did you leave the lights on again?"

"Tool, this is serious."

"Ok. The rain is passed, let's take a look."

The old Beetle had no cover over the engine and it didn't take long for the scavs to see that the fan belt was missing.

"You don't suppose there's a spare in the front? Filler may have one stashed in there."

Frito unlatched the front of the VW and began pulling out the gear that Filler had provided for the trip. Jars of stew, jugs of water, gas cans, a couple quarts of oil, a scissor jack, a length of chain, but nothing resembling a fan belt.

"I got nothing up here. How about you?"

"You mean, did I suddenly shit a fan belt? No."

"How far can we make it without that belt?"

"Not far. Especially while we pull this trailer."

"I thought this fucking thing was air cooled?"

"It is, but that belt turns the alternator, which runs the electrical system. Without it, we'll have to Fred Flintstone this fucker all the way back to Junction."

"So what's the plan?"

"We improvise. Go through everything we got and find something."

The scavs began to rifle through their gear. Emptying their pockets and packs onto the cracked blacktop road. When they were done both men stood and stared at the items.

"What about your pack? Got any duct tape, Frito?"

"No, would that even work?"

"It might. Hey, what's that?" Tool pointed to a red plastic envelope.

"Oh, I found those upstairs at that shop. Figured on giving 'em to Trina."

"Sorry, brother, them pantyhose are getting sacrificed to the Volkswagen gods."

Tool opened the package and straightened the legs of the hose, before cutting them off at the crotch. Then he stretched them out and spun them together like a rope. After that, he strung them onto the pulleys and tied the ends together. Frito watched in amazement as his partner fashioned the makeshift belt.

"You really think this will work?"

"Frito, my boy, I've seen it done on a big ol'

Detroit diesel, back when I was hitchhiking. It worked on that beast and it'll work on this fucking toy. The bad news is, we gotta unhook the trailer and push start her. Then tie the trailer back on."

"Let's do it."

Once the bug was going, the friends hooked up their trailer, repacked their gear and started off again. To Frito's amazement, the improvised belt survived the entire trip back to Junction. As they drove, the scavs did as all men have done throughout time, they told stories. Some were true, some embellished, others completely fabricated, but all entertaining.

"Tool, we've been friends for a while now and I'd guess that I know you better than anyone else in Junction, but until you mentioned hitchhiking, I had never heard you talk about your old life."

"Old life?"

"Yeah. You know. Before everything went to hell."

"You wanna know what my life was like? I'll tell ya. It was shit. My old man was a total prick. I left home just after my thirteenth birthday. Lived on the streets when I wasn't in juvie for stealing or some other bullshit. It was a fucking shit life. Hitchhiking, jumping freight cars, never knowing when I would get to eat, where I was going to sleep, or if I would wake up with some sick fuck trying to put his dick in me."

"Sorry, Tool. I was just curious. I shouldn't have pried."

"All those lousy pricks are dead now, but I'm

still here, still alive, and getting more pussy than anyone in Junction. The sickness was a blessing for me really. "

Frito eyed his friend closely, thinking. "You're fucking with me, aren't you? You asshole. I hate you."

Tool began to laugh loudly, "I can't believe you bought that line of shit!"

"You're a dick. You know that, right?"

"Oh yeah, one of the best."

The Guardian

She loved this place. She had spent many lovely evenings here before everything had changed, before the sickness and death and undead. That's why she stayed. The memories occasionally came flooding back to her. They were wonderful memories of the old days. This place helped her remember. Helped her to hold on to the way things had been, the way *she* had been.

She had loved coming here. Walking down the midway. Listening to the noise of it all. The children running and laughing, squealing from the excitement and sheer joy of it all. She had enjoyed the rides also, of course. The Ferris wheel had been her favorite. Mostly because he had proposed to her at the top. She could remember how much her hands had been shaking. She had been scared that she might drop the ring and never find it below, but she hadn't. She kept the ring even after he had succumbed to the sickness.

The ring was gone now. Lost during her transformation.

Not that it mattered. This place and the home they had shared were more than enough to keep the memories flashing across her mind. That's why she guarded them so fiercely. She knew what the undead could do, crashing around and smashing through windows because their clouded eyes had caught sight of their own reflection. The living were even worse, burning and wrecking things, leaving their stench on anything they touched. For all the years following her transformation she had gladly killed living and undead alike. Allowing neither to get close to those places she held dear. Those places that reminded her that she had once been human. Reminded her that she had once been a normal girl with hopes and dreams. A normal woman with a wonderful man who shared in her interest of antiques. They loved the things they bought and sold in that little store. The apartment above was their love nest. Small and tidy, it was perfect for them.

She guarded these places. Destroying, and often consuming, those who came too close. When necessary, she ate the rats and other small creatures that had the misfortune to stumble into her carnival. It was hers, now wasn't it? Nobody could dispute her claim. Mostly because anyone who might have had long since ceased to exist. A laugh passed her lips at the thought of a courtroom full of undead waving papers at the judge as she sat there in her current form.

The laugh sounded a bit like a cross between nails on a chalkboard and a screeching cat. It echoed around the little trailer and drew her back to reality. She glanced down at her hands, the fingers now freakishly long and tipped with sharp black talons. All her limbs were longer now and covered with oily black skin. Her muscles rippled with every move. It was almost mesmerizing, even to her. Even after all this time, her current form seemed foreign.

But something was different about these two. First, they didn't smell as badly as the others. Second, they didn't break anything, seeming to be almost respectful of the place. She watched them intently as they made their way through her carnival.

Memories of her fiancé came flooding back. His sandy blonde hair and that dirty camouflage jacket she could not convince him to throw away. She missed him still. As the pair moved along she carefully followed them, almost mesmerized by *him*. *He* was special. A bit nervous, glancing around, shifting his weight from foot to foot. She wanted to hold him.

That night, she climbed the wall of her antique store and watched him sleep, making sure to be gone long before the sun rose.

Prophet and Loss

Mitch Burton headed toward the South gate of Junction. He was tired and wanted nothing more than to sit his post in peace. Mitch preferred the North gate, but knew that Earl Pritcher was already there, and wherever Earl was, there could be no quiet. It wasn't that Earl was a horrible person, all things considered, he was probably one of the better people the world had to offer these days, but he just had this thing about prostitution. Not like Tool has a thing about whores, no, Earl was completely the opposite and furthermore he seemed to feel the need to let everyone know just how much he disliked the profession. In the old world, Mitch imagined that Earl had been one of those horrible neighbors who constantly complained about the dandelions in your yard. Probably the head of the local home-owner's association too. He had never bothered to ask Earl about his former life because none of that mattered now, especially not to Mitch who had a job to do.

His job was to keep Junction safe. No small task to say the least. Most days were easy, but when things went to hell, they went in a big way. Zombies weren't a real problem anymore, not many wandered this far out. Even the Sores rarely came close to the walls, preferring to hunt those individuals who were foolish or desperate enough to leave the safety that Junction provided. Pilgrims and scavs were their regular targets and more than a few good people had been lost to those animals. The only real threat to the safety Junction provided was the gypsies, more commonly called gypos by the residents of Junction.

Mitch liked to think of the gypsies as the terrorists of the new world. They tended to infiltrate successful communities in small numbers. Once they got a foot hold, their companions on the outside would storm the gates to rape and pillage, taking what they wanted and burning the rest. Even by modern standards, it was an ugly end.

As he approached the gate, Danni gave him a wave. She was an odd person but she looked quite at home holding a shotgun, most likely a loaner from Filler. She had shown up with a small group of pilgrims a few months ago and decided to stay. Unlike most women, Danni refused to sell herself, choosing instead to do odd jobs, filling in where needed to keep herself fed.

"Hey Danni. How was the night shift? Anything moving?"

"Quiet. Just the way we like it. Tool went out just before dawn, but that's it."

"Good. Have you had breakfast yet?"

"Nah, Filler gave me some stew to get through the night. "

"How about you go get us both something to eat? On my tab."

"You don't have to do that."

"I know, but frankly I'm hungry and too damn lazy to get it myself."

"Alright. Anything in particular?"

"Yeah. No stew. Anything but that damn stew."

Danni laughed at the look of genuine disgust that had crossed Mitch' face.

"How about an order of Eggs over Myhammy with a side of blueberry pancakes?"

"Don't tease me."

As Danni was climbing down from the guard post atop the wall, Mitch picked up the binoculars that hung in their usual spot and began to scan the horizon. Something in the distance caught his eye. Some movement far down the old interstate that lead to their little town. Mitch looked over his shoulder toward Danni as she walked away.

He yelled down to the girl, "Tell Filler we got movement on the road."

Danni gave him a nod before continuing her errand.

By the time they had finished breakfast, Mitch could clearly make out the figure of a ragged looking man with a full beard and shaggy hair. He lowered the binoculars, rubbed his eyes and handed them to Danni. "Take a look and tell me what you see."

"It's a real mess of a man…." She trailed off then added, "Is he wearing a robe?"

"Oh good, you see it too. Thought I was losing my mind for a minute. If you're not too tired, would you mind hanging out until the wizard gets here?"

"Sure thing Mitch."

Sometime later "the wizard" complete with staff, made his way to the gate and looking up at the guards, made a grand gesture of spreading his arms wide as if he meant to open the gates by sheer force of will, "I am a stranger in a strange land. I seek an audience with Pharaoh."

"I'm sure you are." Mitch said loud enough

that only Danni could hear. "I'll go down, you stay here and keep that twelve-gauge ready."

Mitch opened the gate just enough to let the wizard in. "Well, Moses, what brings you to Junction."

"Wan in April the draught of March has pierced to the roota, then longin men to goon en pilgrimages."

"Look Moses, we got enough crazy. If that's all you bring to the table, you can turn right around." Mitch was looking the man over. The old bathrobe was filthy and open enough to reveal more dirty clothing underneath. On his back was a yellow pack, muddy and stuffed to the point of bursting, but no obvious weapons.

"If I were insane, I wouldn't know that I was insane. Since I know that I'm insane, I must in fact be sane."

"Be that as it may, you better have something substantial to offer if you plan to stay in Junction."

"The prime directive forbids me from interfering with the development of those less evolved."

"I'll escort you to Filler's. You can get something to eat and a room for the night, but you better plan on paying for it."

"Very well, captain."

Mitch opened the door to Filler's and pointed to a table. As Moses made his way to a chair, Mitch continued into the kitchen and knocked on the office door. A voice boomed from the other side, "What?"

"We have a visitor."

The door opened and a large figure filled the

frame. Filler was big. Far too big in a time when most were gaunt from fighting to survive day after day.

"What's his story?'

"No idea. So far, nothing he's said makes much sense."

"Crazy?"

"No, I don't think so. Just strange. I got a feeling that he's up to no good, but it's just a gut thing."

"You think he's a gyp?"

"Hard to tell. Maybe just a pilgrim, but I don't like him."

"Alright. Who's at the gate?"

"Danni stayed on. I'm going back so she can get some rest. I'll leave Moses for you to deal with for now."

"He calls himself Moses?"

"No, I came up with that one. You'll see."

"Tell Danni not to forget where that shotgun came from."

Mitch nodded as he walked away. The fat man didn't really run Junction but he sure as hell acted like it sometimes. Mitch kept the thought to himself as he returned to his post.

Filler slowly crossed the gloomy dining hall. Despite his bulk he glided effortlessly between the rickety tables and chairs disturbing neither. As he approached the table where "Moses" sat indelicately devouring a bowl of stew the disheveled man greeted him without looking up from his meal.

"Hail Caesar."

"Filler. My name is Filler. You'll do well to remember that. What's yours?"

"Would not a rose by any other name smell just as sweet?"

"Cut the shit and answer me or get the fuck out of my sight." A ham sized fist landed on the table for emphasis as Filler loomed over the man.

"Names Johnson."

"What brings you to Junction?"

"Twern't Mormons."

"Alright Johnson, just keep this in mind. You're already in my debt for one bowl of stew and unless you want to sleep with the pigs tonight you'd better start making sense."

"The words of the prophets are written on the subway walls. Does Junction have a subway, a temple?"

"A temple? You mean like a church? No. Right after we built this place, this building, people came here to pray together, but the preacher died that first winter and nobody ever took his place."

"Fear is the mind killer. Lay your fears aside for I will bring your people together under one roof, this very roof, that they may know the wisdom of the truth."

"Sure, you will. Here's the deal, Johnson, keep the crazy to a minimum and don't run up a debt you can't repay, we'll get along just fine."

"I shall render unto Filler that which is Filler's."

"I'm sure you will." With that, Filler rose to his full height and returned to the kitchen, stopping briefly to bellow at the serving girl, "Start a tab for

Johnson. I'll want to see it at the end of the day."

That evening as Filler looked over the day's receipts, he paid special attention to Johnson's transactions. The newcomer had eaten two meals and bathed. Not many people took the opportunity to bathe while they were in Junction. To Filler's surprise, Johnson had not purchased any companionship or liquor. Over the years Filler had learned to read people based on nothing more than their purchases. Johnson, however, was not fitting into the standard mold. Unless he had gone to Janet's to fulfill his desires the man was an enigma. Filler made a mental note to keep tabs on him, maybe even talk to Janet.

The next day, Filler was making his usual rounds, checking to see that his girls had been keeping the stills clean, seeing that the hog pens were secure, the garden tended. As he passed through the kitchen on the way back to his office, he clearly heard one of the girls mention something about attending church. He was already in his office when the words finally sunk in. Perhaps crazy Johnson was serious about holding services. He decided to find the man and ask him.

"Anyone seen Johnson?" Filler's voice broke up the trio of kitchen staff who had been huddled giggling near the large stew pot.

One of the girls smiled and pointed to the dining area. There, seated at the table, was a somewhat distinguished man with short hair reading from a thick tattered book and making notes on a single sheet of paper. Filler was instantly angered that he had not been informed about yet another new comer and went to set the fellow straight.

"Hail Filler. The man who doth bestride the narrow world."

"Johnson?" Filler had stopped mid stride. The clean cut, freshly shaven man looking up from his book was the same mess of a human being who had arrived only the day before. "You clean up well for a crazy man."

"Am I? Or are the others crazy?"

"Whatever you say, Johnson. Now, are you planning on having church here? And when?"

"On the morrow, fair fellow."

"Alright then." Filler started to walk away then turned to have another look at Johnson. The man was handsome. His complexion clear, his face bore only one small scar on the cheek which seemed only to add to his good looks. His hair, now brushed and clean, was sandy colored with strands of grey, the bangs hanging over the right eye. It occurred to Filler that some of his girls might be tempted to give Johnson "a freebie."

By afternoon all of Junction was buzzing with the news. The stranger in town would be leading them in prayer and preaching the gospel to anyone who cared to attend. The meeting would be held at Filler's the following morning.

Most of Junction turned up for the services. It wasn't that they were all that religious, but rather that there simply wasn't much in the way of entertainment these days. Stories of the outside world were valued by everyone in town. Even Filler and old doc Shoup were known to accept a decent story as payment for services. As such, an opportunity to hear the stranger talk at length on any subject at all was an event that few were willing to miss.

As people began to arrive at Filler's, the serving girls saw to everyone's needs. Their boss had given them specific instructions. Anyone who came in for the sermon should be pressured into a purchase of water and food. The girls did their best to keep Filler happy. Not out of fear, he wasn't violent with them, it was more out of respect. He kept them safe and few men had done that in this world. That alone was enough to earn their loyalty it seemed.

Eventually the man called Johnson came from one of the back rooms to stand at the end of the large dining hall. He waited there for only a few seconds as the patrons repositioned their chairs then fell silent before he cleared his throat and began to speak.

His voice was loud enough to be easily heard by all. His tone, the inflection, the eye contact, all on a par with the great orators of days long gone. The congregation remained fixed, unmoving throughout the sermon. Not one person dared to make a sound until Johnson had finished, turned and walked slowly back to his little room. Even then it seemed to take several minutes before anyone moved. Slowly the residents of Junction began to rise and make their way to the door.

Once outside, people began to speak of the sermon. Relating their favorite bits.

"He's right you know. What we have here in

Junction is a failure to communicate."

"The beginning was best."

"Tomorrow is another day. We can be certain of that."

"Junction is not the stuff that dreams are made of."

Inside the building, the girls in Filler's employ were washing dishes while having a similar conversation about the wonderful Johnson who had brought with him a "new hope."

Filler was not at all interested in the sermon. In fact, he had not bothered to listen to a single word, choosing instead to remain in his little office. Later, he would judge the proceedings based on nothing more than the day's receipts, just as he based all his decisions. Still, he could not help but hear the excitement in the girl's voices as they went about their labors later that day.

Janet gave a solid knock on the closed door then waited several seconds before knocking even louder. Through the door she could hear the squeak and scrape of a chair and some grunts that sounded a bit like "come in." She opened the door slowly and peered into the little room. Shelves lining the walls were crammed with books. Behind the table, Doc Shoup was rubbing his eye's, glasses pushed up on his forehead.

"Hey Doc, got a minute?"

"Fewer with each passing day, I'm afraid."

"Sorry to wake ya Doc, but I wanted to ask if you had attended that sermon this morning."

"I did." As he spoke he retrieved a second

glass from a drawer and began to fill them both from the ever-present bottle on his desk.

"What did you think?"

"Whaddaya mean?" Sliding one of the glasses toward Janet.

"I mean, all my girls can talk about is this Johnson fella and his sermon. They won't shut up about it."

"And you want my opinion? Well I'll tell ya." Doc emptied the coffee mug of liquor before continuing. "It was horseshit! Absolute horseshit. That man plagiarized every famous book, movie and song known to western civilization, when there was a western civilization that is."

"You think he's crazy?"

"No, but I think anyone who listens to him for long will be. Still, it was entertaining."

"So, I'm told." Janet up-ended the glass, emptying it. "Thanks Doc. I'll let you get back to sleep."

"I was just dozing a bit. Stay for another drink if you like."

"Alright, Doc. One more couldn't hurt." Janet pushed the empty glass towards the old man. He was clearly correct in his statement about having fewer minutes. Old age showed on his creased face and spotted hands. "Think you'll go to any more of Johnson's sermons?"

"Sermon? I'm not sure that's the proper word for what he did today, but if nothing else he does put on a fine show. I'll most likely attend the next one. How about you? Just out of curiosity maybe?"

"Guess it wouldn't kill me to go just once, see

what all the fuss is about."

"Stop by beforehand and we'll toast your new-found dedication to the gospel. Hell, maybe Johnson can convert you. Make you into one of those born-again virgins."

Janet nearly spit her drink out at that. "Dammit Doc! I nearly wasted good liquor. On that note, I best get back over to my place before the girls start pulling hair. Thanks for the drink. Enjoy your nap."

Doc started to protest but thought better of it. He had been dozing a bit and even if he hadn't there was no point in arguing with the madame. Janet was a tough old broad. Doc liked that about her, he thought to himself as he drained his cup one last time before leaning back in the rickety chair and closing his eyes.

Filler had eyes and ears all over junction, mostly in the form of his employees. They were all working girls who typically gleaned information behind closed doors, but not one of them had shared any information about Johnson, apart from stating how handsome they found him or how politely he interacted with them. Not once had Johnson purchased time with a single woman in Junction. At first Filler had thought that Johnson was going to Janet's to buy companionship, but his sources there had confirmed that this was not the case. The man had not once paid for a woman or for liquor in the weeks since his arrival. Johnson ate two meals a day and bathed once a week. Filler gave the man credit for consistently filling the dining hall and certainly couldn't complain about the increased revenue. Johnson, it seemed, was a man of his word. Still, Filler had a bad feeling about the newcomer.

During the week that followed, each of the women in Filler's employ came to him to discuss her account. From experience, Filler knew that most people only became concerned with their financial standings when they were planning to leave Junction. It was not uncommon for a girl to join up with a group of migrating pilgrims and Filler rarely denied a request for emancipation, provided the individual's debt was not excessive. However, to have every one of his employees considering this at roughly the same time was more than a bit unsettling, but then to have Johnson himself knocking on his door, that was more than any business man could be expected to deal with.

"Hail Filler!"

"What do you want, Johnson?"

"I believe that God has planted in every heart the desire to live in freedom."

"That's great Johnson. Still doesn't answer my question."

"I've been locked inside your heart shaped box. Forever in debt to your priceless advice."

"You owe me nothing. You've consistently brought in customers and asked little in return. We're square for now."

"The wage of sin is money spent."

"Save it for the sermon," Filler said dismissively, turning his attention to the ledgers on his desk.

"Debts and lies are often mixed together."

Filler slowly rose to his full height, "Johnson, I don't know what you are getting at, but I'm certain that I don't like it."

"To pay one's debts is honorable. To pay another's is admirable." With that Johnson turned and left the cramped office.

Johnson was giving his sixth sermon in as many weeks. As usual, nearly all of Junction was present to hear the man's cryptic words.

"Rebellions are built on hope." Johnson looked up from his notes then continued, "Freedom is just another word for nothing left to lose."

Murmurs of approval could be heard throughout the room. Heads nodded in agreement. Female heads mostly. Johnson took advantage of the moment to make eye contact with several of the ladies before continuing.

From their location in the kitchen, Janet and Filler listened to the sermon. They could not see Johnson, preferring to situate themselves in such a way as to facilitate watching the congregation. The clear majority of whom were in their respective employ.

As the sermon seemed to near its end, Filler moved to the back door of the kitchen, motioning for Janet to follow him outside.

Once alone, in a voice not much louder than a whisper he asked, "Well? What do you think?"

It took only a second for the foul-mouthed madam to formulate her answer.

"Houston. We have a problem."

Filler's face flushed with anger. He didn't

care much for the proprietor of Planet Janet's. Mostly because she was his primary competition with regards to arranging companionship, but also, because in their years at Junction she had not once been in debt to him. Making light of their current predicament was not going to improve on the relationship.

"Let's meet later, after sundown, at Doc's. Maybe we can come up with a solution to our problem."

"What about Mitch? Do you want him in on this?"

"Good call, but nobody else. People find out we are talking to each other, they are bound to figure out that something is up."

"We could let it slip that we are having an affair." Janet stifled a laugh as she walked away, careful to stay close to the wall and out of sight as people could be heard leaving the dining hall.

Doc's little office was a bit crowded, not because there were four people present, but because Filler was big enough for two men and Janet was not especially small herself. Each of them held a glass. Both Filler and Mitch Burton rarely drank, but Doc was their host tonight and it seemed only polite.

Filler took a sip from his cup and began, "Janet and I have already discussed this, and we agree that Johnson is up to no good. My guess is that he plans to leave soon and take damn near all the women with him."

Mitch Burton had known that something serious was up when he saw that both Filler and Janet were together in the same place. "I'm not sure why I'm here." Taking a small sip from his glass. "If the ladies want to leave there really isn't anything we can do to stop them."

"Mitch, you know that those women are as good as dead once they leave here with that mad man."

"No, Filler, I don't know that for certain and even if I did, it wouldn't change my point of view. Unless they are deep in debt to someone here, they are free to go. It's that simple."

Janet spoke up now, "Look boys. We're talking about losing half the population of Junction. The important half. These girls aren't just whores. They tend the gardens, feed the hogs, work the stills, cook the meals and man the guns when needed. These women are the backbone of Junction. Without them, our little community will cease to exist."

Filler was impressed by the old madam's words. Clearly, she had given this some thought and truly understood the gravity of the situation. Still, Mitch was not swayed.

"I get the distinct feeling that you two are asking me to take part in some devious plot to eliminate Johnson. Well, I'll have no part of it. Furthermore, be damn careful what you do inside the walls. My jurisdiction ends at the gates. If you're gonna do anything severe make sure it happens outside the gates. Is that understood?"

Filler and Janet nodded agreement. Satisfied that he had made his position clear, Mitch placed his glass on Doc's desk and left without saying another word.

"Well Doc, you got any ideas on how we can get rid of Johnson without destroying Junction?"

Doc refilled his coffee cup from the bottle of liquor sitting in the middle of his desk. "Mitch is right. We can't kill the bastard. Least ways not openly. Besides, these poor girls are so warped by him at this point, you may just martyr him and they all leave anyway."

The fat man's facial expression turned from one of determination to weariness as Doc's words sunk in.

Doc continued, "Let's give it a couple days and meet again. I'll do some research. See what I can find in my books."

"I'll drink to that." Janet drained the glass and added," Two days," before slipping out the door.

Filler set his empty glass on the desk, covering it with his hand as Doc again picked up the bottle. "Doc, this is getting out of hand. We can't let him get away with it."

"As it stands, there isn't much we can do about it. Get some rest, things will be clearer after a good night's sleep." Doc leaned back in his chair and put his feet on his desk, his eyes already little more than slits.

Filler spent the day pouring over his books in hopes of finding something he could use to get rid of Johnson. By afternoon his head was throbbing from the strain. He decided that perhaps he should go outside for a while. Maybe spend some time with the hogs. Watching them was somehow relaxing, probably because, "Hogs always make you money."

At this same time, Johnson sat in his room, pouring over the tattered book he held so dear. Reading his favorite parts over and over again. His lips moved slightly as his fingers slid gently over the page. Mumbling quietly to himself, "For Brutus is an honorable man."

Filler was leaning against the hog pen, a fence made mostly of old pallets and street signs when he heard a voice behind him.

"Hail Filler."

Filler turned to face the prophet who was once again wearing his long bathrobe, though it was now clean.

"Nice robe, does that mean you are planning to leave Junction?"

"Men at some time are masters of their fates. The fault, dear Filler, is not in our stars, but in ourselves that we are underlings."

"Johnson, what are you driving at?"

"Wenches cried and forgave him with all their hearts, if Caesar had stabbed their mothers, they would have done no less."

"Johnson, if you are leaving, we can't stop you, but by taking those girls, you are dooming them to die out there."

"And yet you conspire against me."

Filler saw the man's hand flash from his robe, the large knife he held slicing through the air, then through Filler's left forearm as he deflected the blade. Johnson tried to pull back his hand for another stab, but the fat man held it firmly by the wrist. The prophet swung with his left hand now, the small blade in it went straight through his victim's hand as he tried to protect his face. The fat man's right hand closed around his attacker's fist as best it could.

Filler was bleeding heavily from the deep cut in his left forearm and while he outweighed Johnson, the man was freakishly strong. Unable to overpower him, Filler pulled him closer until the tip of the large blade began to pierce his shoulder. Instinctively Johnson tried to pull away and as he did, his would be victim shoved hard, sending the attacker back several feet. Johnson recovered his balance and prepared to lunge again. Filler looked around for something to use as a weapon, finding nothing, he prepared for the next onslaught.

"I come to bury Caesar." With that he lunged forward.

Filler braced himself, not sure how well he could fare. Then, as he stood there bleeding, wondering if this was his end, Johnson's robe seemed to explode as a bullet tore through his chest from right to left. The prophet collapsed in the dirt. Not certain where the shot had come from, Filler went into a crouch and tried to determine its origin.

Mitch Burton lowered his rifle, walked to where the prophet's body lay, removed the large knife from its lifeless hand, then sunk it into the base of the skull and up into the brain.

"Come on, big man. Let's get you over Doc's." Mitch helped the bleeding man to his feet.

"For the record, Mitch, he came at me."

"No kidding? I thought maybe you planted those knives in his hands."

"What were you doing back there? Shouldn't

you be at the gate?"

"I was coming to talk to you. I wanted to remind you that those girls are free to leave if they want. Then I saw you two grappling. Wasn't sure who the aggressor was until you pushed him away and I saw that big knife."

Mitch opened the door without knocking. "Doc, wake up!"

The physician rubbed his eyes and tried to focus on the men. "What happened?"

"The president of the Filler fan club has resigned, it seems."

Doc inspected the wounds then began to rummage through drawers, setting selected items on a tray.

"Care to fill in the blanks for an old man?"

"Our preacher, Johnson, decided to carve the Easter ham a little early this year."

"Yeah, I'll say. Its only mid-March. This is gonna hurt, wanna drink?"

"Just stitch it up Doc." Filler winced as Doc, unceremoniously went about the job of closing the large gash in his forearm.

Mitch watched the proceedings for a couple minutes before asking, "Filler, did Johnson say anything to you, or did he just come out swinging?"

"Just the usual gibberish. Something about stars and fate and wenches. Why?"

"He didn't by chance mention Caesar, did he?"

"He called me Caesar. Did it when he first got here too."

Doc spoke without looking up from his work.

"You know what I think? I think he never planned to leave with them girls. His plan was simply to usurp the throne."

"What are you talking about, Doc?" Filler's words were punctuated with grimaces of pain.

"I think Doc is right. When he first got here, he asked for an audience with Pharaoh."

"That crazy bastard!" Filler had finally caught up. "He didn't just want the girls, he wanted everything."

"Bingo." Doc spoke through clenched teeth as he bit through the thread he'd just tied off. "And as they say, beware the Ides of March."

"Looks like you guys are about done, I'm going back to the gate."

"Hey Mitch, I know we don't always see eye to eye, but thanks."

"Filler, I didn't do it for you, I did it for Junction. It's my job to keep Junction safe. I'll have the body drug out to the pit."

To Be King in the Land of the Dead - Part 1

1

Pacing tight circles on the small right-side platform that stood next to the north gate, Laidlaw looked out over the deserted highway, peering into the distance, seeing nothing but heat shimmer on the badly broken, faded blacktop. "It's bullshit, Burty. I've done plenty for that woman and she can't front me even ten minutes with one of the girls. It's bullshit, Burty. It really is."

Mitch Burton occupied the platform on the other side of the gate. Sitting in the rusty folding chair someone had left there, he propped is feet on the short rail and looked out over the "town" of Junction. He hated being called "Burty", more so because the name-caller was Frank Laidlaw. "Can you blame her, Frankie? I mean damn, after how you tuned up on the last girl I'm surprised she hasn't fed you to that gawdamn cat of hers yet."

"Man, that was just a misunderstandin'. She went batshit, too. Damn cut still hasn't healed up yet." He hiked up the back of his shirt, showing Burton a nasty slash across his lower back, about five inches in length, reddish and seeping. "Hell with that bitch, Burty. I don't need her stinkin' ass whores anyway."

"There's always Filler. He's still got a few girls left."

"Eh, me and Filler don't 'xackly see eye to eye, on, well… nothin'."

"That's because you're a fuckin' shitheel,

Frankie," Burton said. Standing up and stretching he almost laughed out loud at the look on Frank Laidlaw's face. He kept it in though, knowing one of them would end up at Doc Shoup's if he started bellowing at the asshole across from him.

Laidlaw stood with his knees pressed against the low rail, his rifle hanging by its strap. Hands clenched at his sides, he glared across at Burton. With a sudden burst of emotion, he spit out, "Eat me, you damn funker!"

At this Mitch *did* burst out laughing, keeping it in no longer. Then both men began to laugh. Insults had been shared, the moment defused and both men returned to their job, which consisted mainly of staring out over the highway and watching the ugly little town.

Mitch gazed across the town of Junction, eyeing the tiny huts pieced together from tires and tin, wood pallets, brick, whatever a person could find. These huts made up the primary housing of Junction. He could see his, close enough to hit with a rock, sitting squat and forlorn among the rest of the squat and forlorn "homes" spread out on the wide four lanes of the cracked and faded highway. "Damn, I hate this place," he muttered.

"What's that?"

"Just bitchin' Frankie, just bitchin.'"

"What about, Burty?"

Mitch sighed, wanting to tell Frank to stuff it. "Life in general, man. The shittiness of everything."

"Yeah, I hear that," Frankie said. "You know what I think…" Frankie began as he slapped at the sound of a bee buzzing near his hear. It dawned on

45

him after several swipes that that no one had seen a bee or butterfly in years.

Peering down the highway, squinting to see through the heat haze he made out the cause of the buzzing, a shadow in the distance that crept slowly closer. "Well, I'll be damned, he came back."

"Who came back?" Mitch asked. He stretched again as he craned his neck, following Frank's gaze down the highway.

"That kid, uh… Corey's his name."

"Yeah, I remember him. Mouthy little shit, kinda pudgy lookin' in the face."

"Yep, that'd be him." Frank Laidlaw chuckled, "I'm surprised he'd come back so soon, after he and Tool got into it."

"You know how these scavs are, man. Ready to kill each other over a rumor one minute, sharing a whore the next."

"Gotta get your tales' worth of tail somehow!" Frank blew a loud fart and laughed heartily at both his joke and his gas.

"I'll wait up here, you go let him in, check his shit."

Laidlaw nodded, climbing slowly down the shaky ladder.

Minutes later the incessant buzzing became a lopsided humming rumble as the worn-out Vespa scooter Corey Balmont drove pulled up outside the gate.

Frank slid open a small aperture in the larger gate, watching as the man removed the grit encrusted swimming goggles he wore as riding glasses. "Come in slow. Gonna search the cart. You know the drill, kid." He noticed as the man on the scooter stiffened at the use of the word "kid" and chuckled softly to himself.

Swinging the gate in just enough for the scooter to scrape through, Frank stepped back and waited for the small trailer tailing behind to clear before quickly slamming it shut again with a loud clang that echoed through the town. He threw the massive bolt, and re-looped a chain connected to it over a hook welded into the frame.

"Hey there, kid, surprised to see you back so soon." Frankie walked up to the idling scooter, flipping back the tattered tarp covering the trailer. A couple of gas cans, a battered rifle, several water-stained boxes, and an old rucksack filled the minimal space. "Anything good in here, kid?"

"Fuck you, Frank, I'm no damn kid." Corey's voice was raspy from the long, dry ride. "And no, nothing in there for you, butt-wad."

Frank Laidlaw smiled. He usually enjoyed the banter shared with returning scavs, but this kid could get under his skin damned easy. "Get yourself any good ass while you was out there, *Corey*?" Frank made a point of emphasizing the name.

"Damn sure did, Frank! Best I've had in fuckin' ages." Corey smiled at the dark, grinning face looming over him.

"No shit! Well come on, man, don't hold out." Frank's pulse raced at the thought of a good sex story from outside the gates. Life in Junction revolved as much around the tales the scavs brought back as the recovered goods they returned with.

"Yeah, man, it was a couple days out," Corey

said, smiling. "I was at your mom's place. Tapped it hard, Frank. Good stuff for an old woman, I gotta tell you."

Franks eyes darkened, his grin turning down, "My mom's dead, you little prick."

Corey flashed a big smile up at Mitch watching from the platform above. Looking back to Frank he said, "Nah, Frank, you dumb Sore, she's alive, said to give you this." Corey flipped a middle finger up in Frank's face.

Corey's head snapped sideways with the force of Frank's open-handed slap, nearly tumbling him off the scooter. The sound rang out with an echoing crack.

Corey looked back at Frank, then up at Mitch who held his rifle just a little higher. Tears filled his eyes as a thin line of blood traced a path from the corner of his mouth through the sparse stubble to drip from his chin.

"Better learn to watch your shitty mouth boy, gonna get you more than slapped one of these days." Frank glared his disgust and turned around, climbing back up the ladder. He knew if he didn't step away that it would escalate to the point that he beat the dipshit kid to death.

"Go on Corey, head on over to Filler's and check in," Mitch said.

Corey looked up at both men on the platforms and spat an arching gobbet of blood in Frank's direction. The scooter rumbled and buzzed down the street, navigating the shacks, going toward Filler's.

"Fucking kid," Frank mumbled.

2

The scooter wobbled as Corey swiped at the trickle of blood leaking from his mouth. He probed at the inside of his lip, feeling the cut his tooth had left when that bitch Frank slapped him. "Make you regret that, bastard," he mumbled into the wind.

Pulling up to the back of Filler's place he turned off the key and set the little bike on its kickstand. Grabbing a box from the trailer, he pushed through the back door, into the kitchen area.

He sat his box next to a large duffel bag lying on the floor in front of the door to Filler's office. Someone, Filler he assumed, had scratched "Filler Only" into the wood of the door.

Corey eyed the tally sheet to see if anyone had checked in recently, a sinking feeling in his gut when he saw that both Frito and Tool had been in. He hoped they weren't still inside.

Taking up the pen hung next to the list he started to scratch a notation in a spot by his name when he realized someone had crossed through *Corey* and written *bitch-boy* above it.

He scowled but didn't bother to fix it. "Shitheads, every last one of them." Seeing Tool again might not be so bad, he really felt like telling someone off.

He was glad to see that Frey dude wasn't here. Though he would never say it out loud, that guy scared the shit out of him.

Stepping through the doors out onto the dining floor he saw Frito and Tool sitting at one of the rickety, scarred tables. He walked up, wiping away the drying blood on his chin and signaled to the girl now bringing three glasses and a pitcher of water to the table that he would pick up the bill.

"You were gone for a while. How'd you do?"

Frito glanced at Corey as he rooted around in his jacket, producing a bag of corn chips, which he proceeded to dump into his bowl. "Not as good as I'd hoped. I'm going to owe Filler forever at this rate. Everything to the north is tapped out for at least sixty miles."

Tool and Corey both had their doubts about that but left it alone. Each scav chose whether or not to mislead those he competed against. It was part of the game.

"What about the Sores, did you see many?" Tool asked.

Corey tuned out the conversation, letting the two talk. His mind wandered back to his exchange with Frank at the gate. Inside the twists and turns of his thoughts he formulated a plan to get a bit of revenge.

Corey rejoined the conversation when a large shadow passed over the table. "Fat prick." Corey thought as he looked up at Filler. Without preamble Filler asked, "Who wants a job?"

Corey waited to speak, having learned from past experience that volunteering for a "job" from Filler could mean just about any damn thing. He listened as Filler bitched about pregnant whores and how much it cost him. Though his ears perked up when the big man mentioned something about getting his bill wiped clean.

Corey was shocked when Tool burst out with,

"You've lost your mind!" Speaking to Filler like that was tantamount to asking for a nasty death. Even he knew that.

Fast, far faster than anyone would ever expect from such a big man, Filler snatched up Tool, yanking him face to face with a fistful of his jacket. Corey was even more surprised when he witnessed a small, wickedly pointed blade appear from the folds of Tool's jacket and come to rest under Filler's wobbling chins. Corey's mouth opened, a snide remark ready to tumble out into the air and risk his life. He snapped his jaw shut, wisely choosing silence over smart-ass.

The air hung thick with tension for a moment before Filler opened his hands, slowly releasing Tool. "Look, those pilgrims that passed through a while ago said there was a small town with two gas stations about ten days south just off the big road. Those gas stations will have rubbers in the men's rooms. Probably 400 or more."

"Filler, you don't know that for sure. Those pilgrims probably made the whole thing up just to pay you for their room and meals." Frito declared.

Cautiously, Corey said, "Seriously. You didn't accept that bullshit as payment did you Filler?"

Filler explained about a map, and his certainty that there was a town out there. Corey saw on Frito's face that he wasn't interested in the job at all. Waiting, letting Tool have first crack at the job, Corey wasn't let down, besides, he wasn't in bad shape, as far as what he owed Filler. A few simple runs and he'd be clear.

Filler and Tool shook on a deal and everything went back to normal, which was mostly tense uncertainty.

Enjoying a few drinks with the guys, his animosity for Tool buried like the little blade hidden somewhere in the man's jacket, Corey laughed, shared a few stories and ate before standing up on stiff legs.

"Where you heading to?" Frito asked.

"Eh, Gonna go see Janet, I found a little something she might like. Then I think I'll go talk to Doc Shoup."

"Filler's friggin' stew making you sick already?" Tool said around a mouthful of the stuff.

"Oh hell no, I love that shit," Corey said with a straight face. "Nah, I need to go see Doc because I got this nasty rash on my cock, Tool." Reaching for the fly on his worn and patched jeans he said, "You wanna see it?"

Tool flicked a spoonful of brown broth at Corey, "You are just nasty, man!" He said with a laugh.

Corey danced backward, a smile on his face and darkness in his heart. No matter the camaraderie he shared with the other scavs or the residents of Junction, he despised them all. His smile was always false, his joy at another's success was manufactured. He did what he had to survive, and sometimes, just a little more.

Frito lifted a hand as Corey walked away, heading out through the kitchen door, to the back where his scooter waited.

Crossing over the highway to the motel

sitting almost directly across the four lanes from Filler's, Corey flicked a glance up at the guards on watch. It didn't miss his notice that Burton virtually dismissed him by looking away, and Laidlaw spit over the rail, an unmistakable sneer on his face.

Corey felt his guts twist with an urgent desire to climb Laidlaw's ladder and pound his face until he looked like a freshly killed funker.

Parking between the faded yellow lines in front of Planet Janet, Corey shut the scooter down and rooted in the messenger bag slung over the back of the bike. Pulling out a thin plastic case he slipped it inside his jacket and headed for the door.

Whenever anyone opened the front door of Planet Janet a bell sounded that was far too cheery for this town of the barely living. It always set Corey's teeth on edge.

Bibi "Janet" Reno, the short, stocky looking woman with a massive bosom and an attitude far larger came out of the proprietor's door behind the counter.

"Heya, Janet."

The woman's eyes narrowed darkly, staring across the dirty entryway. "Why you little shitbird," Janet said.

Corey flinched when her hand dropped below the counter and his line of sight. He began to back toward the door he just entered. Hands up, pleading, he said, "C'mon Janet! Damn, I thought this was settled."

"Settled my dirty ass," she growled. "You ran outta here too fast for me to catch you last time." Janet came around the counter, advancing on Corey, a hunting knife gripped in her right fist.

"Janet, please, it was a misunderstanding! The bitch bit me! I told her not to bite!" Corey's voice began to rise with feigned terror.

"And you broke her nose, fractured her cheekbone, and busted out two teeth, you Sore-sucking prick. You know how much I owe Shoup just for the fix-up, not to mention hardly nobody wants a busted-up girl, Balmont!"

Janet was close now, almost within arm's reach. "I brought you something, Janet, something that'll make up for it, I promise."

The woman paused, the scar along her chin flaring red in her anger. "Brought what, boy?"

Reaching slowly into his jacket, Corey pulled out the slim plastic case between thumb and forefinger and held it out to her.

Janet snatched it from his fingers and examined the item.

Corey let his hands fall as the knife drifted downward, the red arc of Janet's scar quickly fading to normal. He watched as she flipped the case open and pulled out the shiny disc, checking it for scratches.

"Johnny Cash. Damn, kid, where'd you find this?"

The sheer pleasure on the woman's face told him everything he needed to know. "Just got lucky," he said. "Found it buried under a pile of crap some Sores had been living in."

Janet looked up, awe in her eyes. "You killed some Sores for this?"

"It was just a few of 'em, and I got the drop,

caught them sleeping."

Janet just nodded as she turned back toward the battered check-in counter. Going behind it and reaching underneath, Janet pulled out a portable disc player, small speaker, and a battery pack she kept charged with one of the solar chargers campers and hikers used to favor.

Corey smiled as she slid the disc into the machine and started it up. Soon the voice of the Man in Black issued from the speaker.

The speaker was worn and the sound thin, but it was a sound that pleased Janet greatly. Her smile grew as her eyes closed, lost for a moment in the sound of a life long forgotten by most.

Corey stood silently waiting, allowing the usually bitter woman to revel in the music. Several minutes later she clicked the player off and stored everything under the counter once again. "This doesn't square us, Corey, but it damn sure puts us on better footing. I'm not saying there's going to be a next time, right now, but if there is you best keep your hands on her tits and not pounding her face, you get me?"

Corey nodded solemnly. "Yes, ma'am, Miss Janet, I do understand."

"Now, if you find any more you bring them to me, screw Filler and what you owe him. A stack of these and I'll sell you your very own whore, Balmont."

"Sure thing, Janet, you got it." Corey stuck out his hand, and Bibi "Janet" Reno shook it as firmly as any man.

He kept to himself that he had several stacks

of the compact discs hidden away within twenty miles of Junction. He knew he had something Janet wanted. He also knew Filler wanted her little music setup. Besides, owning a whore was too much responsibility.

"Well, I'm outta here Janet, thanks for not stabbing me," Corey said with a smile as he reached the door.

"Oh hell, I wasn't gonna stab you, Corey."

"Sure looked like you were," he said as he pulled the heavy door open.

She had been gazing at the disc, no doubt waiting for Corey to leave so she could listen without his annoying mouth around. Looking up she gazed directly into his eyes. "Nope, I was gonna cut your throat."

Corey stared back briefly before stepping out and letting the door close behind him. The draft from the door set the large globe hung in the window to spinning lazily, the neon-pink spray paint on it spelling out "Planet Janet" reflected light off glitter that had been sprinkled onto the paint, twinkling as it turned back and forth.

Corey took a deep breath, calming the rapid stomp of his heart. "Fuckin' filthy whore-pedaling whore," he muttered. "Cut my throat? Cut MY throat?" he mumbled aloud as he straddled his scooter, starting it up.

Doc Shoup's place was just down from the motel, sharing the same broken building as Trina's school and daycare. "Daycare my ass," Corey chuffed as he pulled up in front of Doc's.

The storefront furthest from the motel had

collapsed some time ago. It looked to Corey like another building just beyond it had exploded, causing damage to the nearest building. Doc's place was what had been the center store, and Trina's sat on the end closest to the motel, making it easier for Trina and the girls when it came to dropping off and retrieving their kids.

Corey could hear the sounds of chattering and screaming children from Trina's as he walked up to the Doc's door. "One of them could be mine," he thought. The consideration of it gave him chills. Being a father was something he did not want to contemplate.

Doc sat in a stitched-up cloth recliner, leaning back with a tattered book propped on his chest. He twitched, then sat upright, the book falling aside as he kicked the leg-rest of the chair down.

Slipping on a pair of glasses with a crack in one lens the Doc stood up, brushing crumbs from his shirt. "Hello there, boy. Feeling poorly today? Got an itch that you can't rid yourself of? Hemorrhoids maybe?"

Doc Shoup stood just over six feet, though his shoulders were hunched from years of stooping over patients. His dark, greasy hair was neatly combed and parted down the middle. His long legs and thin limbs gave him a gangly appearance that always made Corey feel ill at ease around the man, as if the Doc would suddenly start bending in strange and terrifying ways.

Few people ever liked coming to the Doc. He'd been known to throw needles at his patients when in his cups, attempting to administer medication from a distance, while chuckling to himself. Then there were the stories that the good Doc would occasionally experiment on the newly dead for unknown reasons.

Corey hoped they were just stories.

"Hi there Doc. No, I'm feeling fine. Stiff from the road, but just fine all the same."

Looking out the window, Doc asked, "How the hell you keep that little thing going? Ain't much gas to be found these days."

"I modified it to run on the souls of the damned, Doc"

Doc looked back at Corey, squinting. "Eh, I suppose you'll find plenty of them out there, huh?"

It annoyed Corey that the Doc didn't find his little joke at least worth a chuckle. "I was wondering if you had any poison, Doc."

"You say poison? What the hell you need poison for?"

"I need to poison some rats."

"What, rats? Why poison 'em, meats no good if you poison 'em, kid."

Corey bristled at yet another reference to his youth, despite being twenty-four years old. He knew it was a veiled slight, just another needle from the pricks in this town, hating him just because he was here. Well, they can piss off and die, he thought.

"I know that, Doc. I'm not hunting the rats. There's this place a ways out from here, three houses set close together, a few outbuildings. The whole place is full of rats, and Sores. Looks like they've been there a while."

Doc Shoup wore a quizzical look on his

weathered face. Corey sighed at the insufferable stupidity of the old man.

"Those brain-dead savages don't know half of what they got in those houses, Doc. My guess is there's all kinds of good shit in there, but I can't get to it. I figure I'll set out a bunch of poison for the rats. The Sores eat the rats, the Sores die or at least get really damn sick. I go in and clear them out. Then it's easy pickin'. I just have to spend some time waiting for it to happen, and time is something I've got a lot of."

Doc Shoup shuffled around the room, favoring his right side. From what Corey had been told, a pissed off patient had broken Doc's ankle a while back. That's what you get for going to see a quack, he thought.

"Yeah, OK, I can see that. I think you're crazy to even be messin' with those Sores, but hey, that's your prerogative."

Damn right, old man. Out loud Corey asked, "So, do you have anything Doc?"

Taking a key from his trousers pocket, Doc snapped open the padlock keeping a battered metal cabinet locked. As he rummaged through the contents of the cabinet, he said, "Yes, I do. Potent stuff, won't need much of it. Gonna cost you, kid."

"Of course, Doc. I got time."

For the next fifteen minutes, while Doc pulled jars and bottles down from his cabinet, mixing ingredients, Corey regaled him with new tales of events that had happened to him on his recent runs. Occasionally he would embellish, stretching the truth and other times he would outright lie, making things up as he went.

Many of those living in the village had not left its walls in years, and the stories that scavs and travelers brought through the gates were the preferred form of currency. In Junction those stories meant life, vicariously. In Junction the tales must be told.

"The saddest was the man I met travelling with his son. They were heading out to Cali, kept talking about some safe haven out there. You and I both know there's no such thing as a safe haven these days Doc, but the boy swore by it. The man told me his wife had killed herself; couldn't handle living in this crazy-ass world anymore."

Doc Shoup cocked his head, looking askance at the kid sitting in his chair spinning stories, some of which he was sure were true and others he knew to be outright lies.

"I'll be damned, that's heartbreaking, kid," he said with a faint lilt of sarcasm. "Here ya go." Doc proffered the bottle, top twisted on tightly. "Be careful with that stuff, boy, it's potent."

"Hey, thanks, Doc, I appreciate it."

"Yep. You find anything in that mess out there I can use, bring it on over here. Supplies could use some topping up."

Corey pushed through the door, casting a nod over his shoulder as the Doc stood, watching him go.

The door clunked shut and Doc stepped over to a bookshelf brimming with tattered tomes. Fingering the spines, he read through the titles and smirked, shaking his head. Out loud he said to the empty room, "I read that book, you stupid cheating shit."

Falling back into his well-worn chair, Doc Shoup picked up the book he had been reading, returning to sleep minutes later, the book once again open on his chest.

Corey spent two more days in Junction before heading back out on another run. He spent much of his time lounging in one of the empty "houses" that Filler rented out to scavs when they were in town, flipping through old skin mags or looking over an old map of the region, plotting new scavenging destinations. He even offered to help Tool on his condom run, though it was more a courtesy than a genuine offer of assistance.

What he had told Doc about the small homestead full of rats and Sores was true, and he was anxious to get started. He pulled out of Junction early one morning, rolling up to the gate and waiting while Mitch Burton opened the gate.

Before pulling away he shouted up to Frank. "Hey, Laidlaw, no hard feelings man." Reaching into his messenger bag he pulled out two worn plastic bottles filled with water. He glanced at the bottles, switched them in his hands and tossed one up to Frank, and handed the other to Mitch. "Some water, on me, guys."

Glancing from the bottle to Corey, Frank shrugged and said, "No hard feelings, kid." Twisting off the top, he chugged a swig as Corey pulled through the gate and away from town wearing a face-splitting grin.

3

Bill Robb plodded down the side of the cracked pavement, following the faded white line with his eyes as he placed one foot in front of the other. Despite the fact that few people drove vehicles anymore, due to lack of fuel, he couldn't bring himself to walk in the center of the wide four-lane. It was just one of those silly little things he was unable to shake from before.

He shook his plastic canteen, dismayed at the last few drops of water left. Saving the water, he let the canteen drop to hang from its strap over his shoulder.

A distant buzz drew Bill's eyes up from his worn-through boots. He could see a speck slowly drawing closer and he stopped to watch. His right hand fell to rest on the weathered grip of his Springfield .40 caliber kept in a drop-leg holster that had seen better days.

Several long, dry minutes later a battered scooter towing a trailer pulled up beside him, the driver tugging up old swim goggles, leaving them sitting on his forehead.

Bill nodded, hand still at rest on his pistol. "Hello."

"Hey there, you heading for Junction?"

"That I am."

"You don't have much farther then. About two miles, I'd say."

"That's about what I figured," Bill said. His voice rasped with want for water.

"You sound like hell, man. How long you

been out here?"

Bill thought before speaking, casting a glance at the sky as if he kept a calendar of days written in the clouds. "Been about ten, maybe eleven months since I was last in Junction."

The man on the scooter glanced at the pack Bill wore. "You must've gone pretty far out. Not much left to scav these days, is there?"

Shifting the pack, which was heavier than it looked, Bill tilted his head, looking at the rider. "Eh, just depends on if you know where to look. Listen, can you spare a swallow of water?"

"Sorry, man, gotta make it stretch. You're not far from Junction, you can get there pretty quick, get all the water you need from Filler."

Bill chuckled, "Son-of-a-bitch is still alive, huh? Yeah, I'll just do that. What's your name, kid?"

Bill took noticed of the dark flash in the rider's eyes when he called him "kid".

"I'm no fucking kid, asshole. Name's Corey Balmont." Corey looked closely at the man shifting on tired feet. "You look familiar. We met before?"

Bill's smile tugged at the deeply puckered scar on his left cheek. He held out his hand, "Bill Robb. We may have crossed paths, Corey Balmont," he said the name with just a touch of sarcasm, "but I think I'd remember you. I get that "you look familiar" thing all the time. Just that kind of face I guess."

Corey ignored the hand, slipping the goggles back over his eyes. "Well, good luck Bill Robb. Shit to do and all that." As he revved the harsh sounding little engine he said, "Don't die of thirst before you get there."

Bill turned to watch for a moment as the scooter and its asshole rider faded into the distance. "Well aren't you just a happy little ray of shit-shine," he mumbled.

He pushed on, a little extra bounce to his step as he drew closer to his destination. Ten minutes later he could see Junction's wall and the heavy gate just down the road. "'Bout damn time," he said to the dry air and glaring sun. Lifting his canteen, he chugged his last mouthful of water.

Once he was close enough to see everything clearly, he was surprised that no guards were on the platforms he knew to stand on either side of the gate.

Hobbling up on aching feet, he could hear raised voices beyond the gate. Had he not been so tired and thirsty he would have listened for a minute before banging on the tall, heavy door.

No one answered his pounding, but the voices became quieter.

"What the hell you want?"

Bill looked up to the man that now stood on the platform looking down at him.

"Scav business. Here to see Filler and take a load off for a bit."

The man disappeared without a word. Bill stood waiting for a full minute before the gate began to swing open just enough to allow him in.

"You been here before, ain'tcha?"

Just past the man, at the base of the second tower lay another man, with a tall fellow leaning over him. Bill could see pinkish foam still bubbling from the mouth of the man on the ground. "Uh, yeah, I have, been awhile though. What happened to him? He asked, gesturing at the foaming man.

"Wait, I recognize you. You're right, it has been a while. Well, you know how things work around here then." Glancing back at the man he would have never called a friend, Mitch Burton said, "Fuck all if I know. Doc thinks he was poisoned."

"Damn, any idea how, or who?"

"Yeah, I think it was that fuckin' Corey kid. Little mouthy ass piece of shit asshole Sorefucker!"

Bill Robb spent much of his time out scavenging, alone, away from the small towns that had sprung up around the Midwest. This instance was one of the reasons why he avoided people; the other was the occasional person that still recognized him, despite the scar, from his days in Hollywood.

Taking a breath, Bill said, "Smart-ass with an attitude, right? I just met him, on the road a few miles ago."

"Little piss-wick better not come back," Mitch said, spitting.

"Well, I'm sorry about your friend there."

Mitch turned around, watching Doc Shoup as he worked. "He wasn't my friend, but he damn sure didn't deserve that."

"Well, uh, guess I'll see you around then," Bill said. He hitched his pack higher on his shoulders and took off at a fast walk toward the old station and diner.

Without turning, Mitch waved a hand over his shoulder at the new arrival.

4

Filler watched as the girls cleaned tables, kept the stew cooking, and did various chores. From time to time he would disappear into his office, only to pop back out later to once again watch the women as they worked.

He was leaning his hefty bulk against a wall, watching, wiping sweaty hands on an old hand towel he carried at all times when he heard the bell over the front door chime.

As the person was backlit by the bright sunlight, Filler could only make out a silhouette until the door closed and his eyes readjusted to the normal dimness of the large dining area.

"Well holy shit, look what kind of ugly the cat drug in, if it ain't old Hollywood fuckstick himself."

"Hiya, Filler. Been awhile. I wish it was longer, but I've got business out this direction."

Filler filled the room with a booming laugh, his belly shaking. "Wish it was longer... Ha! Well hell, Billy-boy, business is why I'm here. That and the occasional piece," Filler said as he swatted one of his working-girl's asses as she walked by.

"Fucking prick," the girl mumbled as she made her way back to the kitchen, which only made Filler's grin even bigger.

"I see you've developed better interpersonal skills with your employees, Filler," Bill said.

"Ha, yeah, they all hate me, like I give a flying shit in a high wind. Come on in and sit down." Sit down came out sounding like one word, sidown.

"You want something to eat? Got a pot of hot stew on."

"It's not the same pot you had on last time I was in here is it?

With a chuckle Filler said, "You just can't get that Hollywood funny-man movie star out of you. Might have to beat it out if you ain't careful there Billy-Boy."

Bill Robb looked at Filler for a moment, a darkness beneath the half-lidded eyes said much.

Filler stopped chuckling, watching the man before speaking again. "Eh, hell, Bill, we're good, you and I. I like you, so how about I get you some of that stew, on the house."

"You don't like anybody Filler, and we both know it," Bill said with a cocked grin. "But, you and me, we do go back a bit, don't we?" Bill rubbed two fingers across the scar several times. Filler took the hint.

Usually Filler would have bellowed for one of the girls to get Bill his stew. Instead, he walked toward the kitchen himself, wanting a moment away from his old "friend".

Everyone owed Filler for something, except for Bill Robb. Bill was the only person Filler was obliged to for anything.

Filler sat a large bowl of steaming stew on the table, maybe with a bit more force than intended as some splashed over the side onto the nicked and faded tabletop. "You said you had business out this way. What kinda business?"

Bill took several bites of the dark, slightly bitter stew before answering. "I'm heading into the city."

No matter how many years he had spent on stage and screen, Bill could not have ever hoped to replicate the look on Filler's fat face.

"Cities are suicide, Billy! Even the craziest Sscavs stay the hell outta the cities!"

"Everything is picked over. There's hardly anything left out there, except in the cities, mostly because everyone's terrified to go in them. There's fuel, food, guns, ammo, you name it, just waiting for someone to come get it, Filler."

"Everyone's terrified to go in them for a fuckin' reason, you bat-shit crazy asshole!"

Bill spooned cooling stew into his mouth, enjoying the feeling of filling his belly, even if the stew wasn't the gourmet food he used to eat off the smooth stomachs of naked women. "There are zombies everywhere, Filler. Just happens that more of them inhabit the cities. If a guy can find a way in and out without getting too much attention, well, that person would be one very rich man by today's standards."

Filler coughed into his hand, his fleshy face turning red for a moment. "You're just full of understatements aren't you, Billy-boy? Cities are still packed full of the dead. No one's been in to thin them out. Hell, I'm not sure you could thin them out."

"Somebody's gotta try, big man. That's just what I'm going to do, try a city. If I come back, you and I could really make Junction something special, Filler, like we thought way back when. If not, well, at least it was fun while it lasted." The heavy sarcasm in Bill's tone was unmistakable.

Filler sat quietly, letting his thoughts turn over what Bill was saying. Standing up and taking the now empty bowl, he said, "Listen, you do what you got to do, Bill, but I still think it's a damn bad idea. It's on you though, so what the fuck do I care? Not a shit, that's what. You make it back with some good stuff, we can deal. Other than that, all I can say is good luck and don't get your ass eaten by a pack of runners, or do, I don't much care. Even though that's most likely what's gonna happen."

Bill nodded at Filler. "Thanks for the vote of confidence, big guy. Now, you got anyplace I can catch up on some rest?"

Scowling, Filler said, "Yeah, there's a couple empties out there. Take this, so folks know it's all legit." Filler dug into a pocket, removing a worn index card with the word's "Rented by Filler" scrawled in a shaky script. He passed the card to Bill Robb and stomped off to the kitchen without another word.

Bill smiled at the wide back of the man he had once saved from a pack of Sores, enjoying the fact that Filler never once mentioned charging him for the hovel.

5

Bill Robb, a.k.a. Billy Robbins, once the third highest paid comedic actor in Hollywood, and star of a handful of box-office smash hits, including the wildly hilarious dark comedy Grandma's Funeral, tossed fitfully in his sleep. Low moans emanated from deep in the man's chest; his body twitching as if pricked by unseen needles.

His nightmares were brutal, violent affairs that often left him covered in sweat, exhausted and emotionally drained. The horror that sleep sometimes brought could be overlooked as a side-effect of the world he now lived in, except for the fact that he had been having them since he was a teenager.

Billy Robbins had pushed back against the horror of his nightmares, and by extension, his life, with humor. Eventually that humor had taken him up on stage, then in front of the cameras.

Though the nightmares still came after his success, he found it much easier to cope, especially when he had enough drugs in his system to overload most people's circuit boards.

He had been clean for just over three years when the dead rose up to eat the living. Yes, he still had nightmares, but after everything he had seen when escaping Hollywood, his bad dreams were just that, bad dreams, no longer affecting him quite the same way.

It was difficult to be as disturbed by night terrors when real life was the very definition of true horror.

Tossing the flimsy blanket to the side, Bill sat up in the cot, shaking his head, flinging sweat out in a salty halo.

"Fuuuuck…" He slurred, reaching for a bottle of water on the floor. After a long drink he tugged out a battered pocket watch, one of the only things that survived his hurried exodus from the hills of stardom and cocaine.

Thumbing the wheel on a cigarette lighter he lit a stub of candle, checking the time by the flickering flame. "Four forty-two," he muttered, "Screw that." Before clicking the cover shut, he glanced at the thin letters engraved on the inside. *Laugh it up, Son. I'm proud of you.* A gift from his father just after his first small film role, the watch was the final tie he had to his old life and the family he had loved, even if he forgot about them until he needed a place to go after rehab for far too many years.

Bill stretched out on the cot, hoping he would drift off, even if just for a while. There was no one to pass the time with at this hour, and per the rules of Junction, the gates would not be opened before daylight.

Just after the sun slipped over the top of the make-shift wall, Bill Robb pulled away from Junction in a battered old VW Beetle he had purchased from Filler for handful of assorted antibiotics, a skin mag, and an unopened bottle of Glenfiddich 18.

The VW was a rattle-trap, more rust than car, but it ran. Having wheels would save at least a week of walking. Finding fuel was always a concern, which made the Beetle especially nice, since Filler had converted it run on alcohol he distilled himself. There were several gallons included, tucked safely in the space under the hood.

Bill kept the car wide open, steering with practiced hands around stalled and weather-eaten hulks, slowing only when he was forced to skirt a snarl of wrecked vehicles or a pack of funkers that blocked the roadway.

Few automobiles traveled the roads these days, with gasoline being so difficult to find. Any place that had stored fuel was emptied within the first few years, making gasoline and diesel fuel a premium trade item. Most gas was now going bad anyway, having sat for so long; even treated gasoline.

In recent years he had seen several vehicles that had been converted to run on wood gas puttering down the road. It was a fantastic idea, with the exception that wood gasifiers tended to explode if not carefully tended, and they were slow, since the wood gas would burn off quickly if the throttle were opened wide. A steady, slow pace worked best.

The countryside reeled away behind him, as the cracked strip of highway stretched for miles, leading him to the hell of a city overrun with the dead.

With no one to harvest them, many of the fields had gone to seed. Corn, soybeans and many other cash crops of yesteryear grew wild throughout the Midwest, tablesful of wild food waiting to be picked and eaten. Except people were afraid to come out this far, especially to work fields where a zombie could appear out of nowhere.

"So much wasted food. Wonder how we could harvest that shit," Bill said to the windshield.

Hours later the city came into view in the distance. One of the benefits of the fall of mankind was air far clearer and cleaner than the few survivors could remember.

Abandoned vehicles began to clog the roadway the closer he drew to the metropolitan area, forcing him to slow to a crawl.

The city he now drove to, like all of them, was now a city of the dead. Full of those that couldn't or wouldn't leave, dying in their homes and on the streets. He stared out through the windshield, watching the skyline creep closer. He knew he would have to navigate the suburbs before reaching the city proper, where he believed there to be everything from gun stores to food distribution warehouses packed with goodies.

Everything a man could want was waiting, if he could get…

Bill shouted as the car was rammed from the left side, rocking on aging springs. *SlamSlamSlam* came rapidly, before he could turn to see the pack of runners bouncing off the car, faces twisted in blind hunger. He grabbed his pistol from where it lay in the passenger seat.

Bill's mind ran through different approaches to the situation, discarding each before settling on a daring plan, but one that would be less likely to draw further attention from the hordes of dead waiting out there.

Returning his pistol to the seat beside him, Bill counted five runners coming at the car. Over and over they charged, keeping the car rocking. He knew how they would react to anything he did.

Instead of cowering inside the car, picking them off with the noisy handgun, Bill slid over into the passenger seat, reached back across to the driver side and quickly cranked the window down.

The first zombie dived in arms first, reaching for the soft meaty morsel inside the hard shell. Bill gripped a large bone-handle hunting knife in his left hand with the heavy blade protruding from the bottom of his fist. Reaching with his right he grabbed the left wrist of the dead thing, pulling hard, dragging it further into the car.

With wicked speed the blade snapped out, disappearing into the creature's face all the way to the hilt. Bill jerked, twisting the blade inside the head, reveling in the snapping noises of the skull fracturing.

The zombie now lay limp, more in the car than out. One of its companions leaned in through the window, over the top of the other. Bill lashed out with the knife again, pushing deep into the eye socket, spearing the soft brain tissue behind it.

Two dead runners lay partially inside the car, leaving three outside, still slamming into the vehicle, bashing at it with clawed fingers.

As Bill watched one of the zombies began to slide around the rear of the tiny car, leaving the other two to bash at the small rear side window.

Turning to face the passenger window, his back to the two dead zombies, Bill rolled down the window about four inches and tapped lightly at the glass.

Hearing the tapping, the runner took two long strides and thrust its arm through the slit Bill had created. Pushing the arm up to prevent the grasping fingers from twining in his hair, he reached down and spun the hand crank as fast as he could. The window slid smoothly upward in its frame, biting into the flesh of the hungry thing's upper arm. Bill continued to push pressure on the window crank, forcing the edge of the window up until it pressed against the bone, pinning the arm in the window.

The zombie's fingers continued to flex, trying to reach the man inside. Bill watched, his knife poised, ready to strike, but the creature tried pulling out its arm instead of pressing its face to the narrow space as he expected.

"Well, fuck you," he grumbled.

Bill spoke softly, hardly able to even hear himself over the clamor the three dead things were making. The zombie trapped in the window opened its mouth, blackened teeth snapping.

"Yeah, yeah, I hear you, jack-hole. Stick your face up against that little gap there, and let me spike you, you nasty bitch."

During the first days, in his escape from Hollywood and all the time he had spent wandering the wastelands of the dead that America had become Bill had seen enough violent, gory deaths to inure him to the nastier side of things.

The sight of the zombie pulling its arm from the window, most likely to try for a better reach, was truly disturbing. With excruciating slowness, the arm retreated through the window, peeling everything, skin, meat, every bit of flesh from the bone as it went.

The denuded bone grated against the window, a hollow vibration rising up that sent chills through Bill from head to toe.

"Uh uh, no way, shit-ball."

The meat of the zombie's arm bunched up at the wrist, preventing it from pulling completely out of the car, the flesh hanging down over now-useless fingers like a long glove turned inside out. Cringing, Bill set the knife down beside him and reached up, grabbed the hand and pulled. The zombie was unbalanced, smashing face first into the doorframe, stripping away flesh from its already tattered lips, exposing the teeth. Reaching down with his other hand, Bill cranked the window down just far enough to let the dead thing's face inside the gap sideways, snatched up his knife and slammed it nearly to the hilt in the center of its forehead.

After tugging his blade free, he pushed the zombie away, watching it tumble to the ground. The knot of flesh around its wrist caught in the spot where the window and the doorframe met, hanging up, not allowing the fully dead zombie to fall away.

"Well, shit."

Bill cranked the window down until the arm finally pulled free with a stomach turning *slorp*.

The two remaining dead had stopped hammering at the window and were now watching Bill as he readjusted inside the car. Both opened their mouth and emitted a high, keening wail.

"Ah, shit."

More would come soon, if they were nearby. "Gotta get my shit outta here."

Outdistancing the two runners wasn't

possible. The roadway was far too crowded, and he was facing into the city. If they trailed him, eventually he would have a full-blown horde of every mutation of the dead in the city on his tail. He had to kill them, and quick.

"Ok, bastards, up close and personal then." Reaching into his pack, Bill removed something heavy, with deeply scarred leather surrounding it. Flipping the item open, he slipped it around his wrist, and slapped it shut. Clicking the two small drawbolt catches closed, Bill held up the leather wrapped iron gauntlet and smiled.

Moving with haste, he opened the passenger door and stepped around the car hoping to get to the runners before they moved toward him.

Both zombies turned to him just as he came around their side of the car, the first lunging in. He allowed the arms to grasp at him, thrusting the gauntlet out as the head came forward. With a clack, the teeth crunched down into the leather, stopping at the iron beneath.

Bringing up the blade, Bill waited until the companion zombie was pressed into the back of its partner. Their weight and unbridled force pushed him backward. They were far hungrier than he.

Bill jammed the blade down, leaving it in the head of the dead that was still latched onto the gauntlet. He now carried its full weight on one arm. The remaining zombie bit at his hand just as it was coming off the knife handle, missing by less than an inch.

"Fucking prick. I got one for you too."

Bill had another blade sheathed on the other

side of his belt. Unable to reach it, he pawed at the Velcro pouch he kept his multi-tool in. Tugging it out, he flipped it open with one hand, revealing needle-nose pliers.

The weight of the one still latched onto the gauntlet dragged his arm down, his bicep burning from holding it up. Faking a grab for the knife with the hand that held the open tool, Bill caused the other Zombie to snap forward, teeth clacking on empty air. He lunged, the tip of the pliers burrowing into the temple of the last zombie.

He could see the violence fade from milky eyes as it fell away, taking his tool with it.

It took him a moment to remove the dead thing from the gauntlet; its teeth were still firmly clamped on, even in death. Yanking free the multi-tool he dived back into the car and shoved out the stinking bodies, wasting not a single second. He drove for another two miles before pulling the car into a copse of trees just off the highway, swearing at the rotten smell the dead had left in the car.

Parked in the trees, Bill was less than a mile from the suburbs. He knew that packs of Runners, Funkers, and plain old zombie dead would start appearing with more frequency. He didn't want to think about other types of virally mutated dead that may be wandering the city, undiscovered until one was munching on his face.

Grabbing his pack, gauntlet still latched around his arm, Bill walked into the woods, angling for the nearest set of houses on the outskirts of the suburbs.

"Well, here goes nothin'," he muttered to the

trees.

The Deal

Frito eased through the gate, his usual camo pack hanging from his left hand, a large canvas duffel bag on his back. He made his way around the back of Filler's and went in through the kitchen area. On the way through he dropped the nearly full duffel by a door with the words "Filler only" scratched deeply into the wood face. One of the kitchen girls handed Frito a bowl of brown stew, the spoon sinking out of sight as he accepted it, before marking the meal on a tally sheet next to his name. All the scavs had a running tab with Filler. The girl didn't bother to ask if Frito wanted a drink. She knew what would happen next.

No sooner had he sat down at a wobbly table than Tool came through the door and joined him. The kitchen girl (Frito had decided to call her Whore One) brought over a pitcher of water and three glasses. Tool told her to put it on Corey's bill. Returning scavs were usually treated to a free drink by the others in exchange for information about their "run."

"You were gone for a while. How'd you do?" Corey asked as he approached the table.

Frito had produced a bag of corn chips from one of the many pockets on his camo coat and was emptying them into the stew with one hand as he fished for the sunken spoon with the other. "Not as good as I'd hoped. I'm going to owe Filler forever at this rate. Everything to the north is tapped out for at least sixty miles."

Tool and Corey had their doubts, but kept

them quiet. It was every scavs right to mislead the competition, even if they were friends and comrades on some level.

"What about the Sores? Did you see many?" Tool wasn't bothered by zombies. To him the people who managed to survive outside the wall were far more dangerous. It was a matter of debate amongst the scavs of Junction.

"None alive. Found some remains that must have been Sores. The zombies had torn them up pretty good." Frito poured some water before digging in to the stew. Around a mouthful he added, "Didn't stick around long enough to do any detective work. I'd guess the Sores were sleeping out in the open and their guard fell asleep."

A shadow fell across the table as Filler approached. He wasn't known for pleasantries and greeted them with a gruff, "Who wants a job?"

All three turned to look, but none said a word. They weren't new to this game and nobody was going to agree to anything until they had all the details.

Filler sensed that it was a stalemate and slowly expanded on the opportunity. "Two of my whores have turned up pregnant and that shit costs me bigtime. The scav that brings in 200 rubbers gets his bill wiped clean."

"You've lost your mind!" Tool nearly spat the words.

Filler was big, too big for this world, but he was quick. A large flabby hand grabbed Tool by the label of his black leather biker jacket and pulled him up out of the chair. Just as he began to draw back his left hand in a clenched fist a look of dawning surprise crossed his sweaty face.

Corey saw it first, as he had the better angle, the light coming through the plastic sheeted windows glinted on a razor-sharp blade just touching Filler's double chin. Tool it seemed was pretty quick also. Just as Corey was about to get off one of his signature smart-ass remarks, Tool whispered, "Filler, move that fist one hair and my debt will be wiped clean anyway."

Filler opened his grip letting both hands relax and slowly fall to his sides. Tool lowered his blade and it disappeared into his clothing.

"Look, those pilgrims that passed through a while ago said there was a small town with two gas stations about ten days south just off the big road. Those gas stations will have rubbers in the men's rooms. Probably 400 or more."

"Filler, you don't know that for sure. Those pilgrims probably made the whole thing up just to pay you for their room and meals," Frito said, stating the obvious as he shoveled the stew and corn chip mixture into his mouth.

"Seriously. You didn't accept that bullshit as payment did you Filler?" Corey was cautious as he spoke, ready for the big man to make a grab at him, but all he got was a dirty look.

"They had an old road map. I saw it myself. Tried to buy the map but they wouldn't part with it. There's a town there for sure. Who wants the deal?"

Frito was in no hurry to go back out. He wanted to recuperate for a few days and possibly run up a tab over at Planet Janet's. Corey was intrigued but felt it in his best interest to let Tool have first shot. Besides, Corey wasn't that deep in debt with Filler and could probably be in the clear after a half dozen easy runs. No reason to risk it out there for twenty days straight.

Tool spoke up with, "I'll take the job, but the deal is 100 rubbers. Anything more goes to credit."

Filler's face flushed. He wanted to smack the guy, but that knife was still hiding in there someplace. Anyway, it wasn't Filler's first negotiation. "How about we split the difference? Bring me 150 and your debt is gone. Credit for anything over."

Tool smiled and extended his hand, "Deal."

Filler walked away without another word. Tool motioned to Whore One to bring them something stronger than water. He figured on running up his tab a bit more before he left tomorrow evening.

Life on the Road

In the dead of the night, Tool slipped out the North Gate, seen only by the groggy gate guard. It was against the rules, but the gate guys knew Tool liked to leave at night and he could be counted on to make it worth their while. He circled around Junction, staying close to the wall to make sure he wasn't being watched by any Sores. By his reckoning they were the worst thing walking, even worse than the undead. Sores may not be much smarter than zombies, but they were devious as hell. They couldn't cooperate with each other long enough to mount an attack on Junction but tended to run in small packs of ten or fifteen and anyone was fair game once they ventured outside.

Corey had offered to accompany him part way, but it was halfhearted and frankly, Tool couldn't figure how the kid had lasted this long. Admittedly the boy must have some skills. Nobody with that smart a mouth could have made it otherwise. Still, Tool preferred to go alone, mostly because he didn't want to share the profits. If he made it back with the rubbers he would be out of debt with Filler for the first time since his arrival at Junction. Besides, if Filler was right and there really were 400 or more condoms out there, Tool figured on trading some to Janet. Hell, maybe he'd have enough to buy a whore outright. Not that he wanted to be responsible for another person, but it made sense from an economic standpoint. He was only human, and a man had needs.

By the time the sun started to peek over the horizon Junction was far behind him. He figured on sticking to the big four lane road. He could move faster that way, perhaps even keep going well into the night. It also made it harder for the Sores to ambush him. They'd have to come from the sides, but if he kept to the middle of the road and stayed alert, he'd have at least some warning. With a little luck he might find a car that he could sleep in. Barring that a culvert would suffice.

Four days in and half his water was gone. A large green sign in the distance read Crooked Creek. When he got to the creek is was little more than six feet wide and a few feet deep but it was flowing and didn't smell bad. He filled the two empty jugs and added a couple drops of bleach from a small bottle he kept in his bag. It was nearly dark and he wanted to get moving. There were footprints in the mud so there were probably Sores in the area. At the very least they had been there recently.

A couple hours later he could smell wood smoke carried on the wind. He moved to the far side of the road figuring the Sores had made camp to the west. If he walked all night and through the next day he could cover enough distance to feel safe. On the other hand, if they caught up to him, he'd be too tired to fight. Drawing on the story Frito had told about the remains he'd found, Tool decided on a new course of action.

He'd hole up in the ditch on the east side of the road for a few hours. When it got late, he'd stow his pack and follow the smoke to the Sore's camp, do a little recon. It was risky, but if nothing else, he'd find out how many there were, get an idea of which direction they were headed.

He awoke in the ditch with the moon high overhead. The smoke smell was weak, that meant the Sores were probably asleep, their fire had burned low. Still, the smell was undeniable and not difficult to follow. After an hour of carefully picking his way through brush he found a dirt road that ran roughly parallel to the highway he'd been following. The moon was bright enough to cast shadows so he used them to stay hidden as he got closer to the camp. Suddenly he could see the embers erupt in flame. Someone had thrown more wood on the fire. A shadowy figure was moving around the camp. Tool was hoping to catch them all sleeping, but at least the flames would ruin the guard's night vision, make it difficult to see him approaching in the dark. He closed to about fifty feet of the camp and hunkered down behind a bush to watch for movement. The guard was sitting near the fire now, probably be asleep any moment.

Sure enough, minutes later, Tool could just hear the deep rhythmic breathing. He crept closer, large knife in hand, as he crossed the twenty feet of open ground. Just ten feet behind the guard now, he could clearly see two figures sleeping near the fire. A woman and a child maybe ten or eleven years of age. These weren't Sores, they were pilgrims! Dammit! Now what? Sneak away and leave them to fate?

Tool opted to wake the guard… carefully. He circled the fire and approached the sleeping man from the front, keeping the fire between them. Tool stood in the open and cleared his throat several times until the sleeper startled and rose, machete in hand. Tool displaying empty hands, "Easy, I'm not armed." Not entirely true, but if things went well the pilgrim would never know. The stranger quickly woke the woman and child who huddled behind him. Tool made every effort to reassure them that he was not a threat. No sudden moves, speaking softly.

They were indeed pilgrims, searching for that pristine community "somewhere up north." Part of a larger party, they had become separated when a pack of Sores attacked them two days past. Tool listened intently asking questions about the attackers, "How many were there? What weapons did they carry?"

There had been a dozen pilgrims in the group, but only four of them were men. Their attackers numbered six, all armed with spears, clubs, or axe. Two of the men had been killed immediately in the ambush. The remaining pilgrims scattered.

There was more that Tool wanted to know. Had they seen a town with two gas stations on the big road? "Yes, that's where we were ambushed. While making our escape we got lost and have been looking for the highway ever since."

When Tool was satisfied that he had gotten as much information as possible he agreed to show the trio back to the big road. He told them to follow the road north for five days. Once they reached Junction, find Trina and offer work to cover their food and beds. "Most importantly", he told them, "stay out of Filler's debt unless you want to remain in Junction."

Before they parted ways, he took them to Crooked Creek, filled their water jugs and added a few drops of bleach.

Tool didn't bother to learn their names. He figured the odds of them making it to Junction at only fifty/fifty. Besides, even if they did make it, they would probably have moved on before he returned.

He pushed hard that day and well into the night. The following morning he guessed he was getting close to the town. Maybe a half-day's walk. Soon he saw a sign reading "Younton exit 256." As he started into a sweeping bend in the road Tool could see a vehicle in the distance with six people moving around it. He dove into the ditch and watched as they circled the van. Nearly all the vehicles he ran across had been stripped of everything useful years ago, so why all the interest? Tool kept low in the ditch and moved slowly, hoping to get a better look but fearing what he might see.

As he suspected, it was a group of Sores. They had converged on the turned over van and were arguing over who was going in. Finally, two were chosen. One approached the double doors at the rear of the van while the second climbed up top to the passenger door with a large rock in one hand, a spear in the other. The sound of the glass shattering was followed by screams from inside.

Tool didn't wait to see what happened to the unfortunate occupants. Most likely the remnants of the group that had been attacked a few days previous. He knew the fate of the hiding pilgrims. It was going to be ugly. The stuff nightmares were made of and frankly, Tool already had plenty of those. Better to use this unfortunate event to his advantage.

As the screams continued, Tool picked his way through the trees on the inside of the curve. It was unlikely that any other Sores were in the immediate area and the ones at the van would be busy for a while. Once he got back to the road he kept to the deep ditch until he found the exit for Younton. The town was not on the highway but was clearly visible about a mile to the west. He sat down and watched the road for an hour to make sure there was nothing moving. Once satisfied, he walked along the edge of the road, ready to dive for cover at a first sign of trouble. A full half mile from Younton he could see the tall, unmistakable gas station sign. The numbers advertising the prices had long been blown away, the large orange *66* faded but otherwise unscathed.

Tool moved away from the road to circle the town before making any attempt to scavenge for things of value. Like most towns he'd seen, this one consisted largely of burned homes, stores with shattered windows, and of course, zombies. The undead were predominately congregated in the center of town but stragglers wandered about the west end near the Campbell's Gas and Grocery.

Returning to his starting point, Tool took a few minutes to fashion a spear with one of his double-edged knives, a six-foot sapling, and cordage from his bag. He then made his way to the 66 station. The restrooms were located on opposite sides of the small block building. The door marked MEN was slightly ajar. When he didn't hear any movement within, Tool carefully entered, switching the spear to his left hand, a large knife taking its place in the right hand. On the far wall was a metal box advertising a variety of condoms. Reaching into his bag, Tool retrieved a short, hardened steel pry-bar. It took about ten seconds to wedge the pry-bar in to the lock and bust it open. Hoping to find the mother lode of rubbers, he swung the cover open to find only ten "French ticklers," fifteen "Jumbo Mudders," and six "Glow Worms." Thirty-one rubbers in all. Nowhere near the 150 needed to clear his debt with Filler.

As long as he was there, might as well check the ladies. He cautiously rounded the back of the block building. The ladies room door was closed and locked. Tool rattled the handle several times and listened carefully for any movement from within. Nothing. Then he had a thought. Carefully he moved to the front of the abandoned station and stepped through the large broken window. Bare shelves lined the walls as expected. Tool searched the rubble until he found a piece of broom handle with a short length of chain, a key attached at the opposite end.

Just as he had hoped, the key fit the lock of the ladies room door. Inside, there was a layer of dust covering everything. On the far wall was a metal box similar to the one in the men's room. Tool closed and locked the door before crossing the small room to break into the metal box. Inside there was a gold mine of tampons and sanitary napkins that would fetch a premium at Junction.

It was going to be dark soon and Tool decided to take advantage of this little cinder block room with heavy steel door. He rummaged through his pack and found a jar of stew that Filler had provided for the trip, at a price of course, and a small bag of corn chips, a gift from Frito. He ate half the stew and finished the chips before laying his head on his pack and falling asleep. It was the first time he had felt safe since leaving Junction, but the resulting deep sleep came with a price. Nightmares fueled by the day's events. Nightmares filled with the screams of pilgrims and the gleeful shouts of Sores on the hunt.

He was up early, just as the sun rose, well rested and prepared to pick his way towards the Campbell's store on the other end of town. Tool wasn't about to take on the large gathering of undead that had been milling around in the remnants of downtown Younton. He decided to move north, skirt the town and come at the convenience store from the northwest. Hopefully that would keep the building between him and the rotting meat puppets.

It was a good plan, but apparently the zombies hadn't got the memo. There were three draggers in back, another four out front. Tool dispatched the slow shuffling undead out back with the spear, being careful to make as little noise as possible, before moving to the men's room. The door was wide open, debris strewn across the floor. Tool immediately moved to the condom machine and started to work on the lock. It popped open to reveal two dozen assorted rubbers. He resolved to have a very serious discussion with Filler when he got back to Junction.

The ladies room was next. The heavy door was connected only by one twisted hinge and hung at an odd angle as a result. Carefully he ducked under the door and looked around. The tampon machine was wide open. It looked like someone had blown the lock with explosives but was probably a point blank gunshot. Tool kicked at the trash on the floor and saw a small pad wrapped in pink cellophane. As he knelt to pick it up something moved in the stall to his left. His hand skillfully drew a knife from its hiding place within the worn leather jacket.

Still kneeling, Tool pivoted to see a pair of frightened eyes watching him intently from under the stall door. In an effort to avoid the slow-moving zombies of Younton, a dog had taken refuge in the ladies room. It was a small, brown, rather sad looking animal in obvious need of food. Dogs were scarce these days. Being hunted by both the living and undead as a source of fresh meat had made them an endangered species. Tool recognized the value of this one and decided to take it back to junction. Doubting that the dog would willingly follow him, Tool planned to win it over with a bit of food. Not wanting to share the meager rations he carried, he decided to search the convenience store.

Back outside the local draggers milled around the gas pumps in front of Campbell's. There had been four earlier but now a half dozen had gathered. Tool stood at the corner of the building and tapped his makeshift spear on the ground to attract their attention. They turned in his direction, then as expected began to shuffle towards him. As each one got near enough he made a quick jab with the spear, under the jaw, through the rotten palate and into the runny brain. As the last one approached, it tripped on the pile of now truly dead that had accumulated a few feet in front of Tool. It grabbed his legs bringing them both down as it fell. Tool kicked hard, pulling his leg free before driving the heel of his boot into the draggers soft skull, splattering gooey grey matter in all directions.

The area now reasonably clear, Tool entered and began to scour Campbell's for anything resembling food. There was nothing of value in the main portion where even the shelving units had been looted, so he moved into the kitchen finding nothing but a few unused pizza boxes. In the back of the kitchen was a door marked "manager." The office was a small room with a desk, filing cabinet, and a mop bucket. Tool was an ace scav who knew that places like this, overlooked by others, could be a real wealth of resources. In the filing cabinet he found four dented cans with the labels missing. The long narrow drawer held several pens and a box of paperclips. In the deep drawer on the bottom right of the desk, were two microwaveable meals and an open box of tampons, apparently the manager had been a woman. All things considered, it was a pretty good haul.

Finding the immediate area zombie-free, Tool returned to the ladies room, opened one of the microwave dinners and slid it to the dog still lying in the stall. It ate every bite then licked at the plastic bowl for several minutes. When it finally stopped, Tool filled the empty container with water from one of his jugs. Again, the dog emptied it. Minutes later the dog inched its way towards Tool and laid at his side. Convinced that he had won the animal's trust, Tool got to his feet and left the ladies restroom with his new companion at his heels.

They made their way back to the first gas station. Even though he had not found near enough rubbers to pay off Filler, it had been a full day and Tool wanted to get another good night's sleep inside the locked bathroom before starting back to Junction. The dog nestled next to him as both slept soundly.

The pair emerged the following morning and saw that the zombies of Younton had been on the move. Perhaps it was just chance or perhaps the draggers had developed a sense of smell. Either way, Tool had no intention of taking them all on. His plan was to use the dense underbrush behind the old gas station as cover for their escape. He had taken only a few steps when the dog began to bark. Tool turned to scold the animal when he noticed that one of the undead had broken from the herd and was loping towards them, accelerating with each step. Bracing his spear against the ground at an angle he hoped would catch the sprinter in the chest, Tool leaned forward slightly to absorb the impact.

His aim was off and the blade went in just below the sternum. The zombie's momentum pushed the spear completely through the stinking creature who thrashed wildly at Tool as they toppled to the ground. Teeth snapped shut on his jacket lapel as Tool fought to get his knife hand free. The dog bit down on one of the zombie's arms and pulled hard shifting the pile of rotting flesh just enough for Tool to wiggle his right arm free and plunge a knife through the back of its head.

Tool got to his feet and ran for the relative safety of the brush. As he reached the cover he turned to see two more sprinters crossing the parking area of the gas station. With the dog leading the way they threaded through the bushes and saplings, trying hard to put some distance between them and the mutated undead. The crashing behind them grew ever fainter. Finally, the duo found themselves on a gravel road. Tool stopped for a moment to catch his breath and listen for the sprinters but could hear nothing but the rapid beating of his own heart.

Looking at the dog, "Thanks for your help back there. I don't even know your name."

The dog stared blankly back at Tool. "How about I call you Maynard?"

They stayed on the dirt and gravel road until they came to the pilgrim camp Tool had encountered on his way to Younton, then headed east towards the highway. From there it was an uneventful five day walk to Junction.

Be It Ever So Humble

Mitch Burton opened the South gate for Tool and Maynard just as the sun was going down. They went in the front of Filler's and grabbed a table near the door. Tool was hungry and in no mood to put up with any shit from Filler. He had only managed to bring back about fifty rubbers, not nearly enough to clear his debt. No doubt Filler was going to be an asshole about it, so Tool decided not to mention the tampons and maxi-pads. He'd hold onto those to barter with Janet and Trina.

One of the girls brought him a bowl of the thick brown stew that seemed to be in constant supply. She looked at Maynard, "Is it eating?"

"No, but we'll need some water."

Filler emerged from the kitchen, all smiles. "You got 'em?"

"Not exactly. Found both the gas stations, just like you said, but between the two there was only fifty rubbers." Tool pulled them from his pack and laid the pile of condoms in the middle of the table. "Hope you're not picky about the brand."

"Better than nothing. Find anything else of value?"

"A couple dented cans, no labels, if you want them."

"Sure, and I'll take the dog too. It's pretty scrawny, but meat is meat."

"The dog stays with me."

"We had a deal, Tool. I supplied you for the

trip. Gave you the information. The dog is mine."

"Filler, the deal we had was for rubbers. Nobody said anything about a dog, but if it will clear my debt, you can have him"

Filler laughed, "You got a fever, boy? That dog ain't worth nothing!"

"Then you won't mind if I keep him, will ya."

It was a tense moment. Filler knew that Tool was serious and no matter how you sliced it, good scavs were valuable. Besides, the deeper in debt Tool stayed, the more control Filler had over him.

"Ok, you keep it, but don't let me see it in here. Ever, or it's going in the stew."

"Soon as I finish this slop, we'll both be going."

Tool grabbed two of the dented cans from his pack, placing them next to the rubbers. Filler bellowed loudly towards the kitchen. A girl appeared and grabbing up the items, hastily retuned to the back. Satisfied that their business was completed for the moment, Filler followed her.

Tool finished the bowl of stew, ordered a second, and ate half before placing it on the floor for Maynard. When the dog had licked the bowl clean, Tool filled it with water from the pitcher. "That should hold you for a while. What say we head over to Janet's? A girl for me and… well, I guess you can watch." Maynard looked at Tool, not understanding, but clearly grateful to his benefactor.

Like Cats and Dogs

Just as he was walking out of Filler's, Tool

ran into Frito.

"Just found out you were back. Wanna get a drink? I'm buying."

"Sure, but not a Filler's. He doesn't like Maynard."

"Maynard? You mean the dog?"

"Yeah, Filler wanted him for meat, but… it's a long story. Let's see what Janet has to drink."

"She ain't gonna let the dog in her place either cuz of that mangy cat."

"Shit. Forgot about that thing. What about Doc's? Bet he's got a bottle of something decent. Besides, I got some stuff he may be interested in."

"Yeah? What did you find?"

"You'll see." A grin spread across his face as he patted his bag.

Walking past Janet's, they both stopped in their tracks looking in disbelief. "Is that Johnny Cash?"

"Not my genre, but sure sounds like it." Tool shaking his head.

"Somehow I don't think Burning Ring of Fire is appropriate for a whorehouse."

"Ok. Now I really need a drink. Come on."

They found Doc asleep in his chair as usual, a book laying open on his chest. Frito knocked on the open door. "Hey Doc, got anything to drink?"

Doc sat up rubbing his eyes before sliding his glasses into place. "I think there may be a bottle around here somewhere."

The scavs exchanged knowing looks. Doc always had a bottle or two of Filler's best stuff. Probably because Filler always owed Doc for treating the girls.

"What brings you boys here? Got the drips again?"

"Not this time, but I do have some things here you might have some use for. Mind if Maynard joins us?" Tool gestured towards the skinny dog at his feet.

"He's welcome, provided he don't drink too much. What you got for me?" Doc smiled.

"Found some maxi-pads. Figured you could use a few."

"That's certainly worth a drink or two. They make good bandages. How many you got?"

"How's a couple dozen sound? Found them in a locked restroom while I was looking for rubbers."

"I don't mean to tell you your business, son, but they don't usually have rubbers in the ladies restroom." Doc smiled again as he handed out the glasses of clear liquor.

"Thanks Doc, I'll remember that for next time." Tool rummaged around in his pack and brought out the individually wrapped pads.

Frito spoke up, "Filler's gonna shit if he finds out you didn't give those to him. You two aren't on the best of terms as it is. What's the story with the dog?"

"Found him hiding from the draggers in Younton." Tool told them the whole story. How he'd found Maynard and how the dog had helped out when the sprinter had taken him down.

"Sprinters? What the fuck? Now they're running? As if those stinking funkers weren't bad enough." Frito was not happy about this latest mutation.

Doc held his hand out to the dog. "Why the hell did you name him Maynard?"

"It was either Maynard or Stinkfist. Figured he looked more like a Maynard."

"Really? Those were the only names you could think of? What's wrong with Spot or Rover?"

"Or Blood?" Doc interrupted. "You know, the dog in the Harlan Ellison story?"

Both scavs stared at him.

"Never mind." Doc decided it was too much trouble to explain. "What else you find out there?"

"Just a few things for Janet. Care if Maynard stays here while we go over to her place for a bit?"

"Sure. He don't seem to be much trouble."

Let's have another drink first." Frito suggested. "Not sure I can fuck to country music while I'm still sober."

Doc filled their glasses again and told them about his recent exchange with Corey. Ending the story with, "I knew the little prick was up to something."

A Planet unto Herself

The little bell sounded as Frito and Tool entered Janet's. They waited just inside the door until the busty proprietor appeared, thankful that Johnny Cash was absent for the moment.

"You boys lookin' for a good time?" she asked.

"Always! But how about a little business before pleasure?"

"What you got in mind Tool, my boy?"

Tool, unlike Corey, took no offense to being called "boy." Janet was respected by most of the inhabitants of Junction, Filler being the obvious exception, and he knew that it was just her way of being friendly.

Tool reached into his bag and pulled out a fistful of tampons. "Got any use for these?"

"Oh, I might have a place for them." She smiled as Frito shuddered at the mental image that flashed in his mind.

"How many you got in there?"

"How many will it take to set me and Frito up with a couple girls?"

"A couple? You ain't sharing tonight?"

"We might yet, the night's still young." Tool winked at Janet.

"You little perverts got a dozen more of them tampons and you can have two girls for the evening."

"Throw in a bottle and you gotta deal."

"Alright, but you're gonna have to share a room and I pick the girls."

Tool glanced at Frito who shrugged, "If you're buying I ain't gonna quibble over *little* details." The emphasis was on "little" and all three shared a laugh at Tool's expense.

"Sounds like a deal to me, Janet."

"Alright, you know the rules. NO ROUGH STUFF! Between that kid Corey and that shitdick Laidlaw two of my best girls are sidelined. Can't afford to lose anymore."

"No worries, Janet. You know us, we're gentle as kittens."

Tool paid Janet and she showed them to a small room with a mattress on the floor and a single chair.

"I'll be back in a minute with the girls and that bottle. Go ahead and start without 'em if you want." Janet's laughter trailed off as she closed the door and headed down the hall.

Filler Up

Filler retreated to his office to update Tool's account. Their original deal required Tool to bring back one hundred fifty condoms. In return, Filler would cancel his entire debt. Filler was still not happy about having a knife to his throat, but it was every man's right to protect himself. Besides, Tool was a good Scavenger. Filler figured he would probably need his services again. He took out his ledger, a water damaged notebook, adjusted Tools balance down by roughly one third before returning it to a plastic milk crate under his desk.

Filler looked around the room. Besides the old table that served as his desk there was a bed of sorts. A real mattress raised off the floor by cement blocks and boards. Under the bed were a couple plastic tubs containing some of his personal treasures. Items that Filler held dear because they reminded him of the life he had before the world turned to shit, before the virus was unleashed on humanity. Among them a scratched up, red toy tractor that looked a lot like the one his father had taught him to drive as a child.

The farm where he'd grown up was fairly typical. Acres of rolling hills covered in corn and beans. A few pigs in a pen because dad claimed, "You can always count on hogs to make money." An old wood barn for storing hay and a metal machine shed for the tractors and combine. Filler recalled jumping from the hay loft or handing his father tools as he worked on the old tractor. He'd had a great childhood. Even the long hours spent baling hay in the hot sun were a fond memory.

Filler wondered what his father would think of him now. How would he feel knowing that his son had become a businessman? No doubt dad would not approve of the women in Filler's employ. Not that he had anything against women working, but prostitution was frowned upon in the rural Midwest. Filler could imagine the conversation and the ensuing argument.

After mother had died, they argued quite a bit. By the time Filler was eighteen they rarely talked at all. Each went about the chores of the farm as they had been doing for years. Both men knowing their roles and carrying them out in silence.

Even when his father got sick, Phillip didn't really talk to him. He brought him his meals and gave him the antibiotics the doctor had prescribed, though they didn't seem to be helping. Phill even moved the little TV into his room so dad could keep up on the weather and crop prices. The news was full of talk about the sickness. How it drove people crazy. Made them violent and animalistic.

Then one night as the ten o'clock news ended, Phillip heard his father shuffling around in the bedroom before heading down the hall to the bathroom. A few minutes later a shotgun blast shook the doors and windows of the old farmhouse. Phillip found his father in the bathtub, most of his head blown off.

In the quiet of his office Filler muttered to himself, "I could have done it for you, dad."

Shaking himself back to reality, Filler decided to check on the girls. He still wasn't happy that two of them were now pregnant, but as long as they kept working for him in one capacity or another he'd deal with it.

Phillip Before Filler

With his father gone, Phil was busy trying to keep the farm going. The price of hogs had dropped drastically when some doctor hypothesized that the sickness was somehow tied to tainted pork. Corn and beans weren't doing well either. Apparently, the whole world was either dead or going crazy.

Phillip made a trip into town once a week to get a gallon of milk and a can of chew. Mostly it was just an excuse to talk to other people, to hear their stories, get some news. The small town of Cassady had never been a booming metropolis but now many of the stores were locked. Most had signs in the window reading "Closed due to illness."

He had just finished dinner one day when he heard the hogs banging around the feeders, making considerably more noise than usual. He looked out the kitchen window and saw Dave and Dorothy Wilson from the farm down the road. It looked like they were trying to get into the pen. They had always been good neighbors. Phil went to see what they needed.

As he approached he called out a greeting "Hello." At the sound of his voice they turned from the gate. It was then that he saw the milky white eyes and blood smeared faces, their clothing covered in gore. The Wilsons lurched towards him as Phil backed away, tripping over his own feet. He recovered quickly and ran to the house for the old Sears twelve gauge rusting near the back door.

After months of watching countless internet news feeds, he knew how to handle the zombie

Wilsons. Phillip used the bucket on the old tractor to scoop up the remains and haul them into a grassy waterway at the edge of the field before dowsing them in diesel fuel. As he stared into the fire Phil realized that it was time to leave the farm.

When in Rome.

It was obvious that the world had gone completely crazy. Perhaps it was time to join in the madness.

The next day Phillip filled both tanks on his father's truck with "farm fuel" from the raised tank next to the machine shed. He grabbed the large tool box, placing it on the passenger seat he fastened it in place with the seat belt before grabbing a few of the larger tools and stowing them behind the seat. With the truck backed up to the house, he began loading the bed with supplies. Food, camping gear, anything he thought might be of use. He briefly considered taking his old football pads but thought better of it.

Once satisfied that he had everything out of the house, Phillip headed into town. The supplies from the house were lacking in ammunition so he figured on stopping by the hardware store. Cassady was like a ghost town. Absolutely nobody was on the square despite it being midafternoon. The door to the hardware store was locked, displaying a "CLOSED. Please come back during regular business hours" sign. Phillip returned to the truck and reached behind the seat recalling his father's advice, "Anytime you work on this old tractor, be sure to keep your crowbar handy." Smiling at the memory he smashed the glass with the well-used crowbar, reached through and turned the bolt. Once inside he headed for the ammo case. Six cases of twelve gauge were loaded onto a Western Flyer wagon along with some one-pound propane tanks for his camp stove and a few miscellaneous items that struck his fancy on the way back to the truck.

For several months, Phillip moved from one small town to the next. Each place was the same as the last. Undead wandered the streets, homes and shops were boarded up, the living that survived were divided into a few easily recognizable categories. Predators, prey, and "non-player characters" like himself. Phillip saw them all.

The prey hid in basements, barely surviving. They hid from the undead. They hid from the living who were just as bad, sometimes worse. The undead wanted only to eat you, to consume your flesh. The predators wanted everything they could take and would stop at nothing to get it. It was especially rough for the women.

Occasionally, Phillip would cross paths with someone like himself. Guys who kept on the move, scavenging along the way, doing their best to not get involved. Encounters with other NPCs were always brief. Information was exchanged on the whereabouts of the predators and the latest changes in the zombies who seemed to be in a constant state of metamorphosis. All of them told him to avoid the cities.

Phillip wasn't stupid. He knew he couldn't keep moving forever. Fuel was getting difficult to find. The only reason he had been able to keep the truck for this long was that it ran on diesel. Diesel has a much longer shelf life than gas. The predators seemed to miss this detail. While the pumps at the filling stations no longer worked, most farms had tanks of diesel on stilts making it possible for him to refuel when needed but even those were empty sometimes.

As the months wore on, Phillip was beginning to wonder if he'd ever see normal people again. Normal people, as if there was such a thing anymore. Then one day as he headed north on a virtually abandoned highway, he could see movement up ahead. The highway was completely blocked off. A tractor and tow truck were dragging cars into position to form a crude wall that connected a little motel, gas station and other small buildings on either side of the divided highway. Phillip watched from a distance then slowly eased his truck closer to the action.

One man, who had been standing guard with a rifle as the others moved pallets and sheet metal into position, broke away and moved towards the new arrival. Phillip got out, shotgun at the ready and waited. The man greeted him, "Sorry for blocking the road. There just isn't any traffic these days, so we decided to take advantage of the buildings and junk in the area."

"What are you trying to do?"

"We are building a town. A safe haven for the few decent people we meet. You're welcome to stay if you are willing to work and treat people right."

"I was beginning to think there weren't any regular folks left in the world."

"Got any skills, kid?"

"Phil. My name is Phil."

"I'm Bill Robb. If you have any skills, we could find a place for you here, Phil. What did you do before the world went to hell?"

"I was a farmer, not much call for that now."

"People still gotta eat. We have some space set aside for a garden and we managed to get a few wild pigs corralled in a pen over there."

"No kidding? Hogs are great. You can always count on hogs to make money." Phillip laughed at his father's words coming from his mouth.

"Not sure I get the joke, Phil."

"What about my stuff? I've got a truck bed full of supplies, things I've scavenged. Don't really feel like turning it all over to a bunch of people I don't know."

"I get it, Phil. Your stuff is yours. If you feel like helping out with something, it's appreciated, but no obligations."

"Alright, Bill. I'll stay and help out for a while. If I don't like the way things are going I drive away. No hard feelings."

"Sounds reasonable to me. Let's find a place for you."

Phil spent his days tending the hogs, working the gardens, and helping with the wall. Water was a big issue, but several men had dug a trench from a nearby creek and diverted it into the ditch that ran along the east side of the community. The water was obviously not safe to drink so several women worked days filtering and boiling it. Phil talked to the women as he filled buckets to water the hogs and gardens. It was getting to be a real problem, but Phil had an idea. One day he jumped in his truck and went to find the solution to their water problem.

It took several days but eventually Phil returned. In the bed of his truck were several rolls of copper tubing, four fifty-five gallon steel barrels, and what appeared to be the plumbing department from a major farm store, including a few propane torches. In a week he had completed the first still and begun to produce crystal clear water. The creek water still needed to be filtered before it went into the still, but it saved the community a tremendous amount of time and effort.

Suddenly Phil was respected by the others. They asked for his input on everything from slaughtering hogs to what to build next. The latter question, he felt, was most important. So far everyone had been building their own little quarters. Small shacks with just enough room to sleep and store a few personal items. Phil suggested they build a large community building. A place where they could meet, share meals. Most agreed and work was begun on a new "public house" that would be available to all.

When it was finally finished the building was large enough to seat nearly fifty people. In the back was a kitchen area with a wood burning stove. Just outside the back door was Phil's still. Each morning the residents would show up at the still before going to their respective jobs. Handing him a couple empty bottles they would say, "Filler up, Phil." His still became the community version of the water cooler from the bygone days of corporate America.

Slowly, more people were trickling in to their

little "junk town." Most were starving. Many had been worked over by predators. All had terrible stories, but few shared them. The safety of the walls, the gates, the guards, helped the new comers feel human again. New arrivals were given an opportunity to clean up and regain their strength a bit before pitching in with the daily chores. Those who didn't pull their weight were asked to leave. Those who refused to respect the other inhabitants were escorted to the gate. Some had trouble coming to grips with the fact that life inside the walls of Junk Town was not the same as life "out there." They were dealt with.

In time, the increased population was such that Phil had to build a second still. His entire day was spent producing and distributing water. He wanted to get a third still going so they could actually keep more on hand rather than just producing safe water on an as-needed basis, but that meant that they would need a way to store it. At Phil's request, a few of the men went out to look for barrels. Eventually they returned with a half dozen blue plastic barrels previously used to hold vinegar. The barrels were plumbed together so that water from the still flowed directly into them. After a few weeks there was just over three hundred gallons on tap at any given moment.

Phil was admiring his handy work one afternoon when Bill Robb approached him.

"Hey, Filler-up-Phil. You sure got this water system down."

"Thanks Bill. It does seem to be working out."

"So what's next? Indoor plumbing? Hot showers?" Bill chuckled.

"I do like the thought of a nice hot shower. If we could get a barrel up on stilts…" Phil trailed off as the mental gears began to turn.

"I'll bet folks here would really go for that. What do you say we go out and see what we can find?"

Phil turned to look at Bill. "You know, it seems like years since I was outside the walls."

"Well, thanks to you, we have enough water in reserve to last a few days. You and I could get out and stretch our legs a bit if you want."

"Let me get a couple people up to speed on running the stills while you see about getting us some fuel for my truck. Then we'll go for a ride."

"Sounds like a plan, Phil. Give me a few days?"

"Looking forward to it, Bill."

It took Bill three days to collect nearly ten gallons of diesel fuel for the pickup. With the walls completed the tractors were not being used much and Bill figured they could justify it for an extended scavenging run. Besides, if they brought back a few goodies to improve morale it would be worth every drop. The residents were getting tired of the smell from the hogs and from one another. The gardens were doing well, but until the vegetables were ready it was just another chore that needed doing. Tempers were getting short all over.

Bill and Phil loaded the majority of their gear in the back of the truck, except for the guns, water and a few MREs from the storeroom which rode up front with them. There had been a little fuel left in the truck. Phil figured that they could cover about a hundred and fifty miles with the fuel they had as he reset the trip meter to all zeros. The gate was opened as a few good natured remarks were exchanged between the trucks occupants and those manning the gate.

They stopped outside the walls and waited as the gate was closed behind them.

"Where we headed, Bill?"

"How about north and west? Gotta be something out that way."

The two were quiet for some time, enjoying the ride.

Phil was the first to break the silence. "So how did the famous Billy Robbins end up in Junk Town?"

Bill kept looking out his window. "We've got to come up with a better name than Junk Town."

"I don't know, it seems fairly accurate."

"When did you recognize me?"

"Took a few weeks to sink in. At first it was just sort of a deja-vu feeling. Eventually it was your voice that gave you away more than your face. I loved your standup bits. Better than your movies in my opinion."

"Do me a favor and keep this between us. That life is over. Hell, that whole world is over."

"What if we built a stage back at Junk Town? Maybe have you do a couple shows a week? Might boost everyone's morale." Phil started to laugh.

"I fucking hate you, Phil." Bill smiled,

shaking his head.

"Gonna make for a long trip. Know any good jokes?" Phil laughed harder.

"Seriously, fuck off."

Five days later, Phil's red truck sputtered to a stop outside the gate. The truck looked rough. Its windshield spider webbed severely, the large steel bumper battered, the grill smashed in and covered in what looked to be blood and bits of flesh. The gate opened slightly as Phil got out and walked around to the passenger door. When he opened it, a semi-conscious Bill Robb slumped over into his arms. Makeshift bandages covered most of his face and head.

More people shoved through the gate as the bandaged man was held up on either side and helped through the gate.

"Let's get him over to the hall. The bleeding has stopped but he needs water and rest."

"What about your truck, Phil?" A voice from the group asked.

"Keys are in it, but you may need to push it in."

It was two days before Bill Robb was up and walking around again. He still looked a bit gaunt but was clearly on the mend. There was a light rain on the fourth day and he decided it would be nice to walk the outer perimeter. It felt good to be upright, pistol strapped in place on his thigh, the weight was comforting. As he slipped through the gate his attention was drawn to the large metallic sign newly fastened to the wall. **Junction pop. 139**

114

"Oh, now that's cake."

The guard from on top of the wall yelled down, "What's that Bill?"

"Oh, nothing. Just admiring the new sign."

"Phil said you would like it. It's about the only thing you guys brought back from your run."

"Yeah, that was a rough one."

"What went down out there? Filler refuses to talk about it."

Bill Robb touched the large scabbed-over wound. "I better finish my walk before the rain really starts coming down. Seen anything in the area that I need to know about?"

"No. Been quiet all day, but I'll keep a close watch until you get back inside."

"Thanks. Appreciate that."

To Be King in the Land of the Dead – Part 2

1

Corey Balmont lay huddled in a depression behind a pile of crumbled brick, watching a group of Sores about seventy-five yards away through a pair of binoculars with a cracked lens.

There were five males, several of which were taking turns rutting with one of the three females.

What he watched was not procreation, or anything so romantic as sex. Rutting was the only term that seemed to fit the greedy, animalistic behavior of the Sores in their throes of violent passion.

Corey shifted in the shallow dip in the dirt, his growing erection pressing uncomfortably against the ground.

"Bunch of horny bastards, aren't you?" he whispered.

Balmont had been watching this group off and on for several months, learning their habits. He knew that after their rutting, several would fall asleep wherever they lay.

Despite the risk of being out in the open, Corey settled in to wait for nightfall. The next several hours would keep him wide awake with tension, knowing he could be found by a random zombie or one of the Sores he now watched.

Waiting, he considered the Sores, what they were. No one was certain, but many speculated that they were yet another form of viral mutation. A more human zombie. Others believed that the Sores had been infected, survived the virus, but that it had basically melted their brains.

The Sores used weapons and tools. Mostly crude, hand-made implements, though they showed some cognitive reasoning by carrying a knife or other man-made weapon. Crude spears seemed to be a favored instrument.

Corey had no idea if they were a result of viral mutation, or survival aberration; he did know that Sores often exhibited characteristics that would be attributed to prehistoric man.

Their sexual habits and tool-making aside, they also showed a cautious respect for fire and an uncanny ability for hunting.

The huge rats that had taken over the farmhouses were slowly thinning as the Sores ate their numbers. Rats were a staple of their diet, although he had witnessed the group eating human remains, as well as the uncommon sight of wild game.

Corey watched through the binoculars as one of the group piled together tinder and kindling, using a disposable lighter to ignite it. He would chuckle quietly, watching the man using the lighter twitch and jerk every time he flicked the wheel with the index finer of one hand while gripping the lighter with the other, as if, even though he knew what would happen, it still startled him.

Corey carefully lifted a bottle of water laying next him in the dirt, cautious not to make any sudden movements that could draw the eye of a distant Sore. He set the bottle back down after a long swig and lifted the binoculars to his eyes again.

Two of the group crawled into a rusted-out car sitting near the smallest house, one in front the other in the back seat, where they would sleep for several hours or more.

Corey waited anxiously for the light to dwindle, imagining what he might find inside the houses. Realistically, they were probably picked clean years ago. Hopefully, the cluster of houses was so far off the main roads that it had been missed by other scavs.

The firelight dimmed to the faintest glow as night crept in, silently renewing one of the oldest fears of man; that unknown thing in the dark.

Unable to wait any longer, Corey slipped the small bottle Doc had given him out of his pocket, swirling the contents to ensure they were fully mixed. From his pack he tugged out a bundle wrapped in a stained old shirt.

Moving as quickly as sight and sound would allow, Corey skirted the camp carrying with him only his knife, the bottle of poison, and the wrapped bundle.

The rats seemed to realize that a sideways canted shed, boards worn rough and gray by weather and disuse, was the furthest point on the homestead from the Sore's camp. They congregated here, and the smell of rat filth caused him to gag as he crept as near as he dared.

Taking a knee, Corey opened the bottle and sat it beside him. Then he took the bundle, unwrapped the shirt, to reveal a white plastic garbage bag. Opening the bag with deliberate care, minimizing any noise the plastic may make, Corey dumped the contents out on the ground before him.

While the smell of the partially devoured cat was ripe and noxious, it was unable to push away the reek of rat. He had found the carcass several miles away, lying amongst the rot and ruin of other animals. It fit his purpose perfectly.

The smell of the cat would quickly draw out the rats. With hurried hands, Corey doused the body with poison, closing the bottle tightly before shoving it into his pocket as he rose to a crouch. Even as he backed away, squeaks and screeches came from the shed. The rats were hungry.

Creeping back to his hideout in the depression, Corey once again settled down to wait and watch.

2

Bibi Reno was leaned back in her chair with eyes half-shut, savoring the sounds of Johnny Cash coming through the tinny speaker when the little round bell tied on a string above the door jangled its merry interruption.

Booted feet clomping to the floor, she sat up and forward with a scowl creasing the corners of her mouth. The girls knew better than to barge in when she was listening to her music unless it was an emergency, so it had to be a customer. She only hoped it wasn't that nasty little asshole that had brought her the CD.

Though Filler siphoned a bit of her business, nearly everyone in Junction and those passing through, came to see her girls. She knew every face that came through more than once, and the man stepping through her door was a new one, and rather ugly at that.

Stopping the music and slipping her player and speaker beneath the counter, Bibi nodded at the newcomer, taking notice of the scarring beneath his milky-colored left eye. "Afternoon, welcome to Planet Janet, best place to find an out-of-this-world lay." She smiled at her delivery of the line she gave each new customer.

"You Janet?" The man growled the question at her.

Nodding, she said, "That I am. What're ya lookin' for today, fella?"

Lanky hair hanging in greasy strands over his face, the man flicked his eyes around the lobby of the dingy motel before answering. "Lookin' for a girl. Big guy over there," he said, indicating across the highway with his thumb, "said you have girls."

"Girls I have, fella. I'm assuming you're looking for a specific type, since Filler has a few girls himself."

"Black hair, thin, big tits, little scar on her right shoulder. Used to go by the name of Lindy."

Bibi watched the man's eyes as he spoke, the darkness in them a stark warning. This man was dangerous.

"Sorry mister, but I'm afraid I don't have any girls fitting that description." Bibi 'Janet' Reno dropped a hand under the counter, resting it lightly on the stock of a sawed-off shotgun. She only had a few shells for it but was certain she could remove his head from his shoulders with just one at this distance, if need be.

"I wanna see 'em, all of 'em. Bring 'em out here." A glint in the dark pits of his deep brown eyes told Bibi that trouble had darkened her doorstep this day.

"Afraid that's not gonna happen, fella. There's nothing here for you, so I suggest moving on." The hand resting on the shotgun now gripped it tightly, keeping it below the counter.

"I think you're lying, whore." He spoke slowly, his voice deepening with an unspoken threat. "Women don't lie to me, ever."

Just as Bibi was about to open her mouth with a sharp retort about being a Madame, not a whore the door behind her opened.

"Hey, Janet, Bella wants you. She says she

thinks she's…" Cassie looked up at the man standing there and took a step back, startled by his fearsome visage.

The door opened to a small room that Janet allowed the women to congregate in when not on duty or over at Trina's. The man flicked a glance at the three women in the room behind Cassie and his eyes widened. "Lindy," he growled, taking a step toward them.

Bibi's skin crawled at the sound of Marian saying "Oh, God… Mitchell!" The terror in her voice was a thing with teeth.

Looking to Bibi, Mitchell said, "She belongs to me. Get her out here, now."

"I don't think so, fella. That girl works for me, but she doesn't "belong" to anybody, least of all a shitbag like yerself."

Mitchell took another step forward, bringing him within an arm's reach, at least in reach of his long arms, of the counter and Bibi.

The sawed-off popped up from underneath the counter, pointing directly at Mitchell's chest. "Back your ass up, mister, right-the-fuck-now! You can walk out or get your shitty carcass carried out to the pit."

Pointing to his whitened eye, he said, "Little bitch did this, she's gotta pay for it. Besides, her ass is mine. Paid good for her, she comes with me." His voice grew heavier, darker with each word.

"Don't give a shit, fella. Get out now before…"

The shotgun was suddenly ripped from her hands. Marian had come up behind her and snatched the gun, lunging forward, the weapon extended in front of her. "I'll never go anywhere with you, you sick bastard!"

Just as the terrified girl pulled the trigger, Mitchell stepped to the side, bringing up a hand as if to ward off the coming blast.

His hand disintegrated to the wrist, becoming a red splotch on the wall several feet away.

The man bellowed his pain and rage, filling the lobby with the roar of a wounded beast. He glanced at the stump of his arm spraying blood, the wonder and mystery of a disappearing hand lost to him amid shock and rage.

The other girls dropped to the floor, cowering as Marian pumped the shotgun, chambering another shell. She wasn't fast enough to end Mitchell before the spouting stump slammed into her face, a ragged tip of bone gouging a line along her cheekbone.

Bibi was reaching down her shirt into impressive cleavage as Marian was rocked sideways, the shotgun clattering to the floor. The noise the woman's head made when it struck the side of counter went unheard, as everyone's ears still rang from the shotgun blast.

Pulling a tiny silver two-barrel derringer from the depths of her brassiere, Bibi took one step, meeting the man as he stooped to grab another of the girls lying on the floor. She placed the gun against Mitchell's forehead and pulled the trigger.

The small caliber round made a noise like a loud clap and Mitchell's head rocked back. The heavy body crumpled slowly to the floor, wrist still draining blood, spattering over several of the girls.

Bibi watched life bleed from the man's clear eye. Hands shaking from adrenaline, she put out a hand to Bella. "You needed something, baby?" she asked, attempting to bring a sense of normalcy back to the situation.

Marian 'Lindy', stirred, moaning Mitchell's name. Her face was slack, eyes dazed.

"He's dead, Janet killed him, Marian. It's ok now."

Marian's glassy eyes focused on Cassie. "Dead?" Pushing herself up to a seated position with her back against the counter, she looked at Bibi. "You killed him?"

"Sure did, baby. Now let's get you over to Doc's and have a look at your head and that scratch."

Marian reached up, wiping blood from her cheek where Mitchell had struck her with his bleeding stump. "Oh, God, I'm so sorry."

Several of the girls looked up at the sound of running feet. Seconds later several people burst in through the door, weapons in hand.

"You have nothin' to be sorry about, baby. He was a bastard, came here hunting you and he got all he deserved." Bibi stroked her cheek, looking into the girls eyes.

Fear, bright and hot, burned in those eyes. "No, you don't understand. His men, they'll come looking for him."

3

Bill Robb crawled through the shattered window of a single-story house and scanned the room. The living room he found himself in was coated in years of dust. Much of the furniture sat undisturbed, slowly rotting away, except for an old recliner lying tilted on its side. A dark, long-dried blood stain spread away from the chair; he saw no body.

Reaching back through the window, Bill retrieved his pack and sat it just inside, in case a rapid exit became necessary.

Taking his time, knife in hand, he made his way through the abandoned home, searching every room. Taking out a well used flashlight, he probed into the depths of the basement, tapping on the top step and waiting for several minutes. When there was no response to his noise-making he went down the steps, flashlight jabbed out ahead, its dim beam cutting into the murky blackness.

The air was heavy with the smell of age and dust and mildew. Thankfully, he detected no odor of rotting human or zombie flesh.

After checking that the few narrow windows to the basement were still intact, he brought his pack down, secured the door behind him, and lit a candle.

He would rest here for the night, in relative safety. Using some of the roll of duct tape he carried to hold them in place he used several pieces of clothing he found in the two bedrooms upstairs to black out the windows.

With the windows darkened, and the candle

stub burning brightly, Bill settled in for a long night of half-sleep.

The undead things that now walked the earth did not fear the daylight. Even though they could be found at any time, roaming the land, hungry, always hungry, they seemed to prefer the night. Pack numbers would increase in size, or they would roam faster and far more freely than during daylight hours.

In his fitful dozing, Bill could hear them passing the house, following their senseless brains toward unseen food.

The night was uneventful, and rest had finally come.

Waking early, Bill listened closely to the world past the windows while eating a breakfast of hard-tack soaked in bitter chicory coffee, and few pieces of jerky. He would have liked to eat until he actually felt stuffed, but that was a long-ago thing that people rarely felt anymore.

Bill cracked the door to the first floor after listening for several minutes, hoping nothing had decided to move in while he had slept in the basement. Relieved that the house was still vacant except for his presence, he stood at the front window for a time, plotting his route into the city proper, which he hoped to make by mid-day.

Finding shelter in the city, where he was certain crumbling tenements and shattered store-fronts housed hordes of the living dead, would be a chore unto itself.

The rusty grating the deadbolt made as Bill turned the lock on the front door set his teeth on edge. Stepping out onto the porch, eyes gazing out over the dry lawns, Bill was hit from the side with enough force to knock him to the floor.

The zombie landed on top of him, teeth clacking together as they snapped at his face. What he first thought was a huge lopsided grin was the drooping flesh of a lone funker. Why it was on the porch, Bill had no idea, his only concern was the snapping teeth, and the loose skin and muscle that now hung down toward his open mouth.

Bill's gorge rose with the oppressive stench pushing its way into his mouth and nose. He realized that if he had waited just another moment before stepping through the door he would have smelled the damned thing.

Despite the rotting nature of this mutation, it was strong, its hunger driving it on. Lying on his side, pressing up with his unguarded hand Bill slammed the gauntlet on his left wrist into the reeking zombie's skull. Rot splattered, the skull cracked, and the smell grew more intense as brain tissue began to well up through the hole.

Bill gagged, the taste of the chicory burning in his throat as it came back up. Spitting it out, into the open mouth of the biting dead he swung his arm again, a solid hit, the crack as bone gave way to iron and leather loud in the stillness of the early day.

The zombie began to slump over, titling face-first toward Bill Robb's wide eyes. "Oh hell no," he muttered, turning so that the limp body fell to the side and off the porch instead of into his face.

"Well shit. If this is how my day is gonna start maybe I should go back to sleep." Groaning, Bill rolled over and into a pushup, before finally righting himself enough to get his feet underneath him. "I need to take some shit out of this pack," he grumbled.

He looked over the edge of the porch just to make sure the thing was dead; the rest of his breakfast came up in a rush.

"What a fuckin' waste." Bill rinsed his mouth with a swig from his canteen and walked down the steps to the grit littered walk leading to the street.

Having spent so much time alone traveling the wild dead lands of America, he had gotten into the habit of talking to himself or thinking out loud. Silence, he knew first hand, was the aide of insanity.

"Well, time to move." He figured two or three miles to get through the suburban area, though if he had any luck at all he hoped to find what he was looking for long before reaching the heart of the city.

He made good time, easing through streets, cutting across yards, occasionally dropping behind a fence or ducking around a corner to avoid roaming gangs of zombies. "Who said the suburbs suck?" he asked the air. Pushing through a gate, he came into a yard he was certain had been immaculately kept when its owners still lived.

Rose bushes bloomed in wild profusion, having grown up the six-foot high trellis, and spread out into the yard itself, although they were beginning to wilt on their barbed stems. The grass, browning from the lack of rain, crackled under his boots as he walked to a tall tree surrounded by several stone benches.

Reaching up, Bill could just touch the lowest limb of the tree. He didn't care what kind it was, just as long as he could climb it. Setting his pack on one of the benches, he opened it, rifled through its contents and pulled out a small spotting scope, once favored by hunters and shooting enthusiasts.

Tucking the scope inside his shirt, he began climbing the tree, feeling his age in his joints as he pulled himself higher. Sitting down and sliding along a thick upper limb, he was able to reach the high roof of the front porch.

Once on the roof, Bill walked carefully to the peak of the two-story house. Standing with his feet on either side of the peak, he took the scope from his shirt and surveyed the neighborhood.

It would be another mile or so before he cleared the confusion of houses and street, but he could see businesses in the distance. Resale or "antique" shops selling junk labeled as Americana for outrageous prices seemed to sit in every other storefront. Clothing boutiques, hair and nail salons, shoe stores and coffee shops, he even saw a store advertising the largest tabletop gaming selection in the state.

Through it all, the zombies. Many of the stores had busted windows, or broken open doors, and the dead of many stinking varieties roamed in, out and around them.

Bringing the scope back toward the coffee shop, Bill could feel himself start to salivate. One of the windows was shattered, wide open to the elements, but he knew that real coffee beans alone, if they were still good, would make him a king nearly anywhere he went.

This is why he wanted to come to the city.

Though the initial outbreak years ago came as sporadic infections, then several years of collapsing society following the full-blown infection spreading nationwide, cities often fell quickly, with outlying areas lasting far longer.

"Too damn many people living in one place." He had lived that rat's maze of city life for many years, believing himself to a part of it, involved in the bustling world around him.

It wasn't until the city fell to the dead that he realized, without his stardom, he was no one, just another peon. The city cared nothing for him, nor did its people, other than to laugh for a few minutes while he cavorted on the screen and stage, helping them to ignore that same realization.

"Yeah, well, it's all gone, and fuck it anyway."

Further along he could see more shops and stores lining the streets, catering to nearly every vice. Tobacco, alcohol, there were three different "vapor" shops within as many blocks.

"Silly-ass hipster bullshit," he said, chuckling quietly.

Glassing the area, he passed over many businesses, until he snapped the scope back, heart beginning to thump. He could just make out the sign for a sporting goods store.

"Oh, now that's cake!" he exclaimed softly. The phrase came from one of his mid-career films; it was the line most people asked him to repeat when meeting him on the street. He spent several more minutes scouting the area through the spotting scope, taking mental note of the thickest locations of zombies.

Back on the ground, donning is pack, Bill moved toward the gate he came through. The heaviest concentration of zombies was in the opposite direction. No area was completely clear, a few always seemed to be wandering somewhere near where he wanted to go.

Going slowly, watching where he placed his feet, avoiding debris that had gone unchecked for ages, he made his way to the next house and the next.

"Couple more blocks," he whispered.

The siding on the next house had peeled away, hanging out, forcing Bill away from the wall. Coming around the corner he nearly walked into a zombie. Without hesitation he stepped up, blade in hand, and buried the knife in the dead thing's temple. It never knew he was there.

Bill used the buried knife to guide the body as it fell, quietly settling it to the ground. He yanked the knife free and had to choke back a cough as a puff of dust burst up from the dry wound.

"What the hell?"

Glancing at his knife, he saw a faint smear of damp goo on the blade, other than that, everything else was dry, bone dry, like the husk of a withered plant.

Kneeling down beside it, casting an eye over his surroundings to be sure he was still unseen, Bill examined the body. Gray and dull, the skin crackled at the touch of his knife like a handful of dry leaves. Large patches flaked away, only to break apart like aged newspaper. The distinct smell of dry-rot filled his senses. Beneath the flaky skin, the desiccated muscle tissue had a hazy sheen.

Bill spat, the dead-dust like ash on his tongue. "Well, that's a new one on me," he said.

Passing the house, leaning against the wall of the next one, Bill watched out over the wide street leading to the businesses. Dead walked the streets, unaware of his presence. He hoped to keep it that way but knew that with the large lawns and wide streets it would be difficult to move undetected.

In the driveway next to the house a Prius sat on rusted rims, the tires having rotted off long ago. In the back window he saw a sticker, wrinkled and warped, still clinging tenaciously to the glass. In a stylized horror script, it read *ZombieCast-Official Radio Show of...* the rest was obscured by a gray-brown crust of brain-matter that splattered half of the back window.

Despite a brief, deep sadness, Bill chuckled to himself. The societal obsession with zombies had been something even he had partaken of. "Hell, I think I listened to this show," he muttered. He had read more than a few scripts for zombie flicks, a few of which he would have been the lead in.

A passing knot of shuffling dead rambled by on the street, never taking notice of the living meat standing in the shadow of a nearby house. Bill checked both ways before leaping out from the house and running.

Several wandering dead blocks away caught a flash of motion as the man traversed the street, darted across a parking lot and swung around a corner into a narrow alley between a hair salon and a frozen yogurt franchise.

No dead were lurking in the alley, and Bill let out the breath he had been holding as he rounded the corner. He knew that he had been spotted, and quickly went for the nearest door letting into a building.

Crossing mental fingers, Bill grabbed the doorknob and twisted. His heart sank to his stomach as the knob stopped in his hand. Twisting harder, he realized it wasn't locked, simply frozen in place by many years of disuse.

From the corner of his eye, Bill caught movement from the direction he had come. The dead that had spotted him were coming around the building, feet shuffling, dead eyes focusing on their prey. "At least there aren't any runners." Squeezing the knob tightly, Bill turned it with strength enhanced by adrenaline. Internal mechanisms scraped and squealed, protesting their sudden torture.

The bolt withdrew, and Bill yanked hard on the door, popping it open, nearly losing his balance in the process.

"Adios, suckers," he said to the advancing shufflers and stepped through the door just as black, rotting hands reached for him from the darkness beyond it.

4

Crouching next to the body, his knees shooting tiny electric jolts of pain thorough the joints, Doc Shoup touched the dead man's neck. "Ayuh, he's dead all right."

"Of course he is, Doc. I put a bullet in his brainpan."

"Don't be sassy, girl. I'm just doin' my job."

Doc groaned as he stood up to lean on the counter, take some of the weight off his aching knees and ankle.

Filler stood next to Marian, arms crossed, a scowl darkening his face. "So, this Mitchell fella," he said as he tapped at the body with a worn boot, "you say he's got men, and they'll come lookin' for him, that right?"

Marian struggled to think through the throbbing in her skull. "Yes, men, eleven of them last I knew."

"Anything you can tell us about them?" Bibi asked.

"They're all bastards, each and every one," Marian said. "Mitchell was the worst of them, which is why they took to following him. They would rob, kill, just wander around, you know?"

"Gypos? You serious, girl?"

Marian, a.k.a. "Lindy" looked up at Filler. "Yeah, I'm serious. They've been at it quite a while; very good at it, you know?"

Gypos were marauding bands moving from settlement to settlement, taking over and using up everything in sight, murdering and raping, moving on when nothing was left. They were considered to be just a step below Sores, and most shot them on sight, if they got the chance.

"Son-of-a… what the hell did you bring here, girl!"

"Now, just a damn minute Filler!" Bibi said. She wasn't about to let someone come down on one of her girls for something she had no control over, especially if that someone was Filler. "It's not her fault she escaped a psycho and came here. We're just gonna have to handle it."

Several others standing around were already muttering among themselves, discussing what had to be done to protect Junction.

"Well good-gawd-damn, ok then." Filler said, looking at Bibi. "Tell you what, Janet; get every able body to my place in an hour for a little meetin'. We got to figure out some way to take these shit-bags out, if they get in here and take over we're all done for."

"We've dealt with worse, Filler," Doc Shoup said.

"Don't I know it, but we're a man down with Laidlaw dead, and he was one of our best distance shooters. Fuck that Corey, I'll toss his screamin' ass into the burn-pit myself if he's dumb enough to come back here!" Filler turned and stomped for the door. "Get everyone to my place, Janet," he tossed over his shoulder before throwing the door open and stepping out.

Janet suspended normal business, sending her girls out to let everyone know that a meeting was happening at Filler's in a hurry. She kept her shotgun with her, and the last few shells she stowed in a pocket.

Peering at Marian, she said, "We're in for some shit, aren't we?"

Marian nodded, tears leaking from beneath closed eyelids. "Yeah, we are. It's been a while, maybe almost a year, since I ran away. Got a good cut in as I ran, but I had to, Janet. I wouldn't have lasted there much longer. I was able to hook up with a group heading to Utah, had them drop me somewhere south of St. Louis. Bounced around until I made it here. I hoped it was out-of-the-way enough that he wouldn't find me."

"Bounced around" huh? No one just bounces around these days, girl. Life outside walls is dumb and dangerous."

"Yeah, well, I did it," the girl said defensively.

Lifting the shotgun from her lap, Bibi said, "These are part of our problem, or lack of ammunition for them. Filler's got a damn arsenal, I've seen it. There's no ammo though. I'd be surprised if there were five-hundred rounds total in all of Junction."

Marian hung her aching head. "I'm sorry, Janet. I really am."

"Don't be girl, nothing you could do. Let's head on over to Filler's and see what we can figure out."

5

Corey shivered in the cool night air. Brilliant starlight cast a faint glow over the landscape, creating a world of fantasy that seemed separate from the hell he normally lived in.

The noise of sick rats squealing had carried over the still air hours before. Now he prepared to advance on the houses and the Sores occupying the area, hoping they had eaten the tainted meat and were now sick themselves.

Moving with care, he crawled toward the encampment of Sores, taking his time, stopping to listen every few yards. Finally, he could raise his head and see the nearest house less than twenty feet away.

Cocking his head, listening, he could hear human groans off to his left. Pushing himself up into a crouch, Corey slid a hunting knife from the sheath hung from his belt and crept toward the noises.

The first Sore he came to was a female, young, probably no more than sixteen or seventeen years old. She was draped in a mix of sun-cured skins and threadbare clothes. Around her neck hung a necklace of diamonds and gold charms alternating with small white bones. Corey had no clue what the bones were, possibly animal but there was no way to know for sure.

Pinkish foam dripped from the corner of her mouth, splattering on the ground, forming a puddle. Her eyes had rolled up into her head, the veined whites bulging. Corey reached out, extended a fingertip and pressed it against one of the dead girl's eyes. The turgid resistance of the orb sent a shudder of obscene pleasure down his spine.

Corey looked up, glancing around, as if he feared someone seeing him in his private moment of pleasure. Leaning in, face close enough to kiss dead lips, Corey looked into the eyes and whispered, "Work to be done."

Emboldened by the dead girl, Corey stepped into the camp proper with an arrogant gait, knife in hand. Bodies lay scattered on the ground near the fire, the bloody remains of partially eaten rats spread among them. There were five near the smoldering remains of the fire, the dead girl made six. "At least two more around here somewhere," he said to himself.

One of the bodies groaned, rolling onto its back, coughing. A gory spume of bloody froth erupted from the man, the heavier drops splattering over his face and shirtless chest.

Corey moved up beside the dying Sore, hovered over him, watching as pain wracked its body. A trembling hand scrabbled across blood-spattered dirt and grabbed Corey's shoe. The fingers turned up, the gesture a cry for help. Spitting, Corey turned his back and checked the remaining corpses around the fire. All were dead, each having drowned in their own fluids. Moving back to the groaning Sore, Corey knelt down and punched his knife through the forehead of the man. He repeated the process with every corpse except the first girl. She shouldn't turn for a while and he wanted to save her for later.

Faint moans drifted to Corey on the lazy night

air. Cocking his head, listening, they seemed to be coming from the smaller house, to his right, the little cottage that people once referred to as the "mother-in-law" house.

Now that he stood on the grounds, he realized that the small group of houses and barns was not a small community. It was most likely a family homestead. Two larger homes, set about a hundred yards apart, and the tiny mother-in-law cottage, with several other outbuildings made up the full spread.

Following the moans of suffering, Corey made his way cautiously into the tiny house. Another of the Sores had collapsed just inside the door, its body still and cooling as he laid a hand on it.

The moans came again, louder inside the house. Stepping over the corpse, Corey took a second to spike it in the head before moving along the short hallway that led to the combination kitchen/living area, the bath and the single bedroom.

He found the woman in the bathroom, lying inside the old, chipped claw-foot bathtub. The bloody foam had poured from her mouth, over heavy, naked breasts into the base of the tub where it pooled around the plugged drain. He couldn't be sure, but he thought this was the one the males had been rutting with as he watched earlier.

From his count, Corey was certain this was the last of the Sores inhabiting the area. "Hey there sweetheart," Corey said. The Sore's eyes rolled in their sockets to focus on the sound of his voice. "Got yourself in a bad way, huh?"

The woman reached for him, baring her teeth. Even in her suffering the savage rage still drove her.

She had no strength left and her arm fell, slapping the side of the tub.

"That's it, babe, just give over to it. You're dead, sweetheart."

Her eyes seemed to track his face as he spoke. Corey shivered when she suddenly locked eyes with him. Her bloodshot gaze seemed to bore directly into his soul, discovering his darkest secrets. She could see his murder of Frank Laidlaw. She could see his half-hearted offer to help Tool on the condom run for what it was. Part of him had hoped Tool would accept, so he could take the smooth, deadly fucker out of the picture, if given the chance.

Her gaze carved away his mask, ripped at the façade he wore like a tailored suit of skin. "Fuck you!" Spittle flew as he screamed at the dying Sore. He took two steps forward, knees pressing against the rim of the tub. The woman's hand flailed weakly, fluttering against his legs and crotch.

Corey brought the knife down again and again, slamming it into the woman's skull, burying it to the hilt each time, all while screaming "Fuck you, fuck you, fuck you!"

Corey's knife hand stopped in mid-air, hovering there as he stared down at his handiwork. The Sore's head was nearly gone, most of what it had contained now covering Corey, dripping from his knife hand, the tip of his nose, soaking the bulge in his jeans.

Spitting into the open skull-cavity, Corey stepped back and said "Fuck you" once more, this time whispering the invective.

Sitting on the toilet, using the outer curtain

hung on the shower to wipe the gore from his face and arms, he took time to collect himself, settle his mind. Several minutes later he stood up and began the work of scaving, starting with the blood-soaked bathroom.

He found several bottles of pills in the medicine cabinet, as well as a pack of adult diapers beneath the sink, confirming his hope. The place hadn't been picked over yet.

"Well thank goodness for big fuckin' favors," he said aloud.

He went about the business of scaving, forgetting about that first dead girl.

6

Quickly slamming the door shut behind him, hoping to prevent the outside zombies from getting in, Bill shoved at the dead thing grabbing for his face.

With the heavy door closed the darkness was pervasive, almost a physical thing that pressed against him much as the zombie was attempting to. He could see nothing in the thick black of what he thought may be a storeroom in the hair salon.

Bill snapped his head to the side. A sound like a rattling cough came from in front and just to the right of his position. Digging into the left front pocket of his worn khaki cargo pants, he felt and gripped the small disposable lighter he kept for starting fires. Holding it up in front of him, while scraping his feet backward along the floor, he flicked the thumb-wheel.

A bright spark flashed and died, leaving him seeing spots. He flicked the wheel again, and again a startling flash, with no flame. "Shit"

The rattle-cough came again, moving closer. The pitch-black murk revealed nothing.

Before he realized what was happening, Bill was going over backward, a strange feeling, time like warm taffy, stretching and stretching, enveloped him. He felt like he had fallen through a wormhole into infinite space, to fall forever in darkness. Then the second was over and his back twitched in pain as he struck the side of something firm, jamming a point in his pack into his back, just before his tailbone hammered the floor. He couldn't be certain, but he thought he heard it crack.

He still held the lighter in his left hand, the same arm he wore the heavy gauntlet on. Flicking it once more, the lighter flared to life, the small flame illuminating the zombie less than a foot away from him, its body already leaning toward his fallen form.

Before he could react, the zombie came down on him, less like diving, more like a severely uncoordinated fall right into his face. He shoved out the arm wearing the gauntlet. The force of the dead thing knocked the lighter from his hand, darkness refilling the hole the little light had carved in it.

Pressing up, the gauntlet of iron and leather buried in the neck of the beast, Bill pushed back against the insistent force of raving hunger. Reaching down with his right hand, Bill gripped the handle of a knife and tugged.

He realized that the odd half seated position had pushed the pommel of the knife against his thigh, catching it in the cloth of his pants. Several frantic tugs later, enveloped by darkness and fighting to keep the zombie from getting any closer to his face, Bill knew the knife wasn't going to come free.

Hand scrabbling on the ground beside him, Bill's fingers wrapped around something, and released it just as suddenly. It felt prickly, and furry and strange in the blackness, and his heart leapt in renewed terror.

Unseen teeth snapped above him, the sound sharp, distinct, as if he could hear far better than normal. His arm began to ache from the strain of keeping the dead thing off him. It was only a matter of seconds before he would no longer have the strength to fight it back.

Slapping the floor, his heart drumming to make Keith Moon jealous, he grabbed the prickly thing, squeezed tightly, and slammed into where he was sure the head of the zombie was.

His aching arm and shoulder jerked with the impact and he nearly let the diseased thing fall. Drawing back in the dark once more he drove the prickly device hard into the skull once, twice and again, his arm jerking lower each time. "Fucking die you bitch!"

Whatever he was holding had crawled forward in his hand, and he could feel his grip slipping. With one last swing, twisting arm, shoulder and body as much as he possibly could he put every bit of strength left into punching through zombie skull into zombie brains.

With a sound like a thick dry stick being broken skull cracked and the prickly thing pushed into brain tissue.

Bill tried to guide the dead weight of the body away from him, but he had nothing left in his arm. The zombie slapped down onto his chest, pinning his arm between them.

The zombie smelled of dry-rot and dust, making his sinuses feels tingly. "Another Husker," he muttered into the darkness.

Unable to wait in the dark for another second, Bill rolled sideways, his pack catching against the side of whatever he had fallen into. Pushing with his right hand he was able to flip the zombie off him and sit up.

Pulling his pack off and around, Bill unzipped a pocket on the side and pulled out another lighter and a candle stub he kept stowed away. After closing his eyes, he flicked the flame to life, opening his eyes slowly. Lighting the candle, he held it over the zombie.

"Yep, another husker. Damn, you things are a sight." Dry, flaking skin, patches missing, muscle showing. Moving the flame higher Bill began to laugh.

"A damn hairbrush, are you kidding me?" Protruding up from the doubly-dead thing's head was a round bristled hairbrush, one used for styling. Bill laughed until he hurt, bleeding out terror and tension with each laugh.

Banging outside the door brought him back to the moment. There were still dead outside, and their noise would only bring more.

As he was looking up toward the door the hand holding the candle had dipped, bring the flame close to the dry zombie on the floor. The skin caught fire with a puff of gray smoke, and the body began to burn like it had been soaked in oil.

"Oh, shit!" Bill jumped up, grabbing his pack and slinging it over a shoulder. The body burned hot, bright and fast, flames reaching a full foot in height within seconds.

"Ok, this ain't good." Blowing out the candle, Bill stuffed both lighter and stub into a pocket and looked around for a door.

Across the room, through a maze of boxes labeled with various hair product logos, Bill could see a door and he made for it quickly.

Stopping beside one of the boxes, Bill popped the top open and grabbed three of the long green bottles inside. "Son of a bitch," he said looking back at the body, which was now catching nearby boxes on fire. Just this one box of shampoo would be worth its weight in gold.

The shampoos, conditioners, and soaps in this one shop alone would have been enough to make him a King in the land of the dead.

With one last glance at the brightly burning zombie, Bill turned and hurried away, intent on finding a way out before he too went up in flames.

7

Bibi sat at one of the worn and nicked tables, feet propped on another chair. Nearly every seat was full, and nearly every face was a mask of anger.

"Why don't we just give 'em this girl and be done with it, if that's all they want?"

Bibi opened her mouth, her barbed wit ready to sting. Filler caught her eye and glared a wordless warning to let him handle it.

"Because, Earl Wayne Pritcher," Filler began, using the man's full name like a slap across the face, "We ain't ones to just go handin' girls off to their deaths. Besides, these boys are gonna be out for revenge on the lot of us, I'm thinkin'."

Earl sat back in his chair, effectively chastised.

From a woman seated at one of the tables near a plastic-sheeted window, "What do we have to fight the bastards with then?"

"That's why we're all here Andi, to figure something out," Filler told her.

"You say that there's only about eleven of them, or around that?"

Filler looked to Marian.

"Yes, from the last I knew, there were only eleven, but there could be more now," Marian told the room.

"Then what's the big damn deal?" Mitch Burton asked.

"Whad'ya mean, Mitch?" Filler said.

"We got a town full of people, and most of us are pretty handy at stayin' alive. I just don't understand why everybody's getting so bent outta shape over eleven people."

Marian spoke up before anyone could reply. "Because, Mitch, these guys won't just come in here and kill people. They enjoy murdering, raping, that's how they get their kicks, and how they survive. They'll do things, nasty things, just for fun."

"We've all faced some pretty brutal shit, but from what Marian here has told us, these Gypos wrote the book on brutal," Filler said to the room. "We are gonna have to be ready to meet that with the same kind of violence. You folks think you can handle that?"

The room filled with mumbling voices, people talking in their own little groups. Heads bobbed in agreement. "It's Junction, Filler. We're gonna do what we have to."

Filler nodded. "Thought you'd say that, Earl. Everyone needs to keep their weapons handy until this thing is done. Get your guns, if you have any. If you need some ammo, come see me, we can work out something." Even now, Filler wasn't about to let something go entirely for free. If nothing else, he'd keep a record, make sure anyone who couldn't pay, owed.

"We're gonna need more men on watch, both day and night," Mitch said.

"Was just gonna tell you to handle that, Mitch. Get together as many as you think you'll need. See if you can't round up some binoculars; get a few guys posted up all around the wall, not just at the gates. We wanna see what's coming before it gets here."

Mitch nodded in reply, his stomach sinking with the new responsibilities he had been handed since Laidlaw's death. "I'd rather deal with zombies," he muttered to himself.

People began to drift out, some stopping to talk in small groups, working together to prepare for whatever was coming.

As Bibi passed him, Filler said, "Hey Janet, you think those girls of yours will be able to help out?"

Bibi eyed Filler with undisguised contempt. "Of course they will. They're more than just mattress-backs, Filler."

Filler nodded, glancing around the room, watching as people left. "Well, you know I got that little basement here, more of a tool storage and sump area, than anything, but it's solid concrete walls. Got a thick steel plate bolted to the back side of the door. Figured on using it as a hidey-hole if the need ever arose."

"That's nice, Filler, what are you getting at?"

"You let your girls, anyone with children, know to bring them here, when things start gettin' hot that is. We can hide 'em down there. 'Bout the safest place I can think of for 'em."

Bibi grinned, "Well I'll be damned, Filler. There *is* a heart buried in there somewhere beneath that hard ass and flabby gut."

Filler cocked a tilted, sardonic smile at Bibi. "Fuck you Janet, you just see it gets done."

"That I can do. You may want to get some water, and other supplies down there, if you haven't already."

Filler nodded in reply.

Bibi walked to the door, following the last of the stragglers out. Stopping with the door held open she turned back and letting her guard down just the tiniest bit she looked Filler in the eye and nodded, her voice sincere and unusually free of sarcasm. "Thanks."

Wordlessly, Filler returned her gazed for a heartbeat, then turned and strode for the back and the security of his office and apartment.

8

Corey finished his second pass-through of the house, the mother-in-law cottage and the shed, leaving no corner or nook unchecked.

Not finding as much as he'd hoped, but happy with the haul, he packed the tiny trailer, tying a frayed tarp over the top to make sure he lost nothing on bumpy roads.

Just as he was reaching down to unzip his pants and relieve himself on the ground next to the wagon he heard a soft rustling in the grass behind him. Spinning, pulling his knife at the same time, he was shocked to see the first girl he had come across in the camp coming quickly toward him.

Her mouth hung open, foamy pink drool spilling over bluish lips. Her gait, though slightly lopsided, was quick. Corey felt certain that in time she would have become one of the sprinter types, able to cover ground rapidly.

"Well, damn, sweetheart, seems I forgot all about you. I sure am sorry for that."

The dead girl was only a few feet away now, and Corey braced himself, letting her come to him. He pushed aside the thought that if he hadn't heard her footsteps in the grass she would have been chewing on him before he could have reacted.

Flipping the knife over to hold it blade up in his fist he readied himself for the lunge he knew would come when she got close enough.

Three steps away the zombie lunged forward, propelling herself toward her first fresh meal. Corey raised an arm, palm out, arresting her movement with one hand on her left breast.

She continued to press forward, against the hand. Corey's face seemed to split in two with a huge grin. "Oh, now that's nice, sweetheart," he said, flexing his fingers.

Her arms outstretched, reaching for the face wearing the lecherous grin, the dead girl emitted a weak moan.

"Yeah, I know it's good, but I've got places to be sweetheart. No time to dance today."

Corey swung his fist up, the knife slipping in underneath the girl's blood-soaked chin, pushing up through her mouth and deep into her brain. Steel glinted between her teeth.

Yanking the knife free, Corey let the body drop with a heavy thud. He bent over, wiping the blood from his blade on her filthy skins.

"Better luck next time, babe." Spitting on the dead face, Corey chuckled, turned and mounted the scooter.

The Vespa started up roughly, its small engine sounding weak, tired.

Steering the scooter and trailer slowly down a washed-out path that was once a graveled road, he turned right on the cracked blacktop. He would take some time before going back to Junction, heading first for his nearest fuel stash, then take a roundabout way back to the settlement.

"With any luck those bastards will be a little more forgiving by then," he muttered into the wind.

9

The fire continued to spread, rapidly engulfing the single-story hair salon. The bright flicker and the roar of the flames drew zombies from every direction. Soon the building would be surrounded by the idiot dead clamoring for their turn in the blaze.

"Better get a move on, Billy-boy." Bill watched through the front door for several minutes before making his way to the back door. Bill felt a tightening, sick feeling deep in his guts when he saw the heavy steel bar threaded through four brackets, two mounted to the back of the door, one on each side of the frame, a long padlock dangled from a hole that passed through the right-side end bracket and bar.

"Well shit on your security! Damn it!"

Returning to the front of the store, Bill hitched his pack higher on his shoulders and peered through the filthy glass of a large front window hung with various signs.

Outside, beyond the glass, zombies began to shuffle and run and limp from every direction, all heading for the burning building Bill now stood trapped in. Even if he dared to attempt it, busting through the door and pushing through the growing horde would be a death sentence.

Bill wiped at the oily sweat that had begun to bead and drip down his face. The salon was getting hotter by the second. A fluttering terror began to beat feathered wings of dread inside of Bill. He knew if he didn't push out of here in a hurry that he would end up a gibbering, burning idiot crisping on the floor like a lasagna forgotten in the oven; red, bubbling over, spreading out to a puddle that blackened to a hard crust.

Bill shook the image from his mind and cast frantic eyes around the main shop, the tilting chairs, sinks along the wall, bottles of hair products lined neatly on shelves, coated in dust.

A loud crash came from the back room, where he had killed and inadvertently lit the husker on fire. "Fuck!".

Staring for a moment at the rows of hair gels, shampoos and other products, Bill shrugged his shoulders at the half-formed and ridiculous plan that had taken shape in the fevered part of his mind that thought he might still escape the rapidly closing walls of this nightmare.

Grabbing a canvas tote-bag printed with the name and logo of the salon hanging from a rack near the front register, Bill rushed to the nearest shelf and grabbed every bottle of product he could stuff into the bag.

Once the bag was full, Bill set it on the front counter and stacked the bottles neatly, so they stood in tight rows, then he removed all of the caps. Upending one of the bottles over his head, he let the thick, slick goop run down his face. He poured some on his shoulders and arms, then tossed the empty bottle aside.

Catching movement from the corner of his eye, Bill looked around to see several flaming dead round the corner from the store-room, shuffling their way toward him even as gobbets of melting flesh dripped from their bodies.

The sight of a walking fire-ball, teeth clacking, mouth opening wide in a silent roar, burning arms out and grasping, was enough to spur Bill into action.

Snatching up the bag of open hair products, Bill made for the front door, flipped the bolt open, (silently thanking God that it wasn't an internal keyed lock), flung the door open, and stepped out into the crowd of the dead gathering in front of the store.

Yanking a bottle from the bag, Bill held it behind him, squeezing the scented soap out onto the ground as he continued moving through the crowd. Bottle after bottle, whipping them back and forth, he created a slippery path in his wake.

Fingers scrabbled at his clothes as the odors of death and the scent of honeysuckle and kiwi battled for supremacy in his sinuses. Hands squeezed his arms, slipping off easily with a tug. Fingers, some rotting and black, others with flaking skin, tried to get a purchase in his hair, and on his face; they too slipped away.

Bill tried to draw a deep breath, but the overpowering smells shoved reeking fingers down his throat. He retched as he moved, what little he had in his stomach splashing onto his boots. He continued to push on through the horde.

Time had stretched its deceitful membrane around the moment, and the hours it took to get to the edge of the horde and past it were in fact only seconds.

Bill pulled the last bottle from the tote-bag and turned to squeeze the thick fluid on the ground he had just walked over. Lifting his face to the advancing zombies Bill dropped the bottle. Despite the harrowing situation he still found himself in, Bill was unable to contain his laughter.

In a bizarre St. Vitus' dance of the dead, zombies shambling along the trail of goopy hair-care product he had spewed on the ground twisted and slid, arms waving uncontrollably, feet slipping and twitching and sliding out from underneath them. Several of the zombies were runners, sprinting into the muck, feet suddenly flying out behind them as they went face first into the ground, sliding into the legs of others that were still upright, bowling them over.

Blood and other unknowable fluids began to mix with the stuff Bill had laid down, creating disturbingly artistic multi-hued whorls and streaks.

Several undead began to press in from his sides, avoiding the slippery sludge. Still chuckling, Bill said, "Time to move on. Adios, suckers."

Stepping over a pile of trash on the curb, several slower zombies trailing him, Bill made a beeline for the open door of one of the coffee shops, hoping to find refuge, either in or beyond the two-story building. It had not escaped his notice that the buildings along this side of the street were all two-stories, eliciting a twinge of hope.

Broken glass crunched beneath his boots as he swung through the door, moving quickly. The smell of water-rot and stale coffee hit him immediately. "Oh, damn! I want real coffee!"

Toward the back of the shop, stepping over dry, molding bones and scattered debris, Bill made his way toward a door he hoped led up to the second floor.

"Need just a bit of a break here," he told the door as he grasped the handle and pulled.

The door popped open with a bit of effort, the wood swollen from years of damp and heat. Behind him glass crunched.

Several of the dead, including a funker and two huskers, pushed through the doorway, unwilling to give up on the meal that was attempting to get away.

"Sorry, dead-heads, ol' Bill isn't on the menu today."

Bill stepped through the door into semi-darkness, slamming it behind him.

Reaching back and unzipping a small side-pouch on his pack, Bill felt around for a moment, until he located the thin, flat shape he was looking for. Zipping the pocket closed, he ran his thumb over the surface, flipped it over in his hand, and felt for the tiny round button.

The tiny key-chain light glowed in the dark, creating a halo and narrow beam for Bill to follow. Bill shrugged. "Better than nothing, I guess."

To his left a set of stairs went up into darkness, which he began to climb. He was unwilling to explore the downstairs storerooms with just the little light to guide him.

Another door stood open at the top of the stairs, and Bill went through it as fast as possible, leading with the light in one hand and a knife in the other. Standing in an empty hallway, Bill swiveled his head, watching both directions.

He stood in that spot for several minutes, watching, listening, hearing and seeing nothing. Following the tiny light to the left, Bill came to the first of four doors, two on each side.

Opening the first, light from windows that looked out onto the street filled the room. Pocketing the flashlight, Bill stepped carefully into the apartment, closing the door behind him.

The odor of human decay hit him like a fist. Sneezing and gagging simultaneously, he dug a handkerchief from a pocket and pressed it to his face, blocking both his nose and mouth.

Taking shallow breaths through the material helped, and he continued on into the apartment. The large, open-floor plan of the main portion of the residence allowed Bill to see most of the kitchen, living and dining areas all at once. He saw nothing that could be giving off the nauseating smell.

To the right was an open door, leading to what he assumed would be a bedroom and bathroom. The bathroom was to the left, and it too was empty.

"Just leaves the bedroom." Bill turned to face the next open door, the corner of a bed visible. "Damn, I don't wanna go in there."

Drawing a breath, Bill stepped into the bedroom. The handkerchief was unable to block much of the odor, it being strongest in here. Watering eyes quickly scanning his surroundings, Bill saw nothing until he stepped around the corner of the bed.

"Oh, fuck me," he gasped, backpedaling.

In all the years since the zombie apocalypse had begun, Bill had never seen anything like what lay on the floor before him now.

The woman, her dress rotted to tatters and shreds, lay on the thick carpet. Her eyes rolled loosely in their sockets, and Bill could see the glistening muscles working. One of the thin strands of muscle connected to her left eye popped free as he watched.

The zombie's body twitched, and jittered as it tried to sit up, to reach out for him. The mouth opened, facial muscles glistening blackly as they constricted. No sound came from the woman.

Shock locked his knees. Bill stood there staring, his eyes wide in disbelief. "Holy shit," he whispered without realizing he was doing so. "How long you been here?"

The zombie's body had to have lain in its position for years, though it was impossible to tell for how long. Most of the skin, as well as some muscle tissue had rotted away, puddling around the body, acting like a putrid glue, sealing the living corpse to the carpeting.

As he stood watching, the thing tried to tear its left arm up from the thick ooze. A squelching sound somewhere between sweaty sex and violent death filled his ears. It was a sound Bill hoped to never hear again.

Slipping his knife free, Bill took two steps forward, knelt down above the zombie's head and punched the blade into the top of the skull. The body stilled, the wet noises silenced. Bill breathed a gagging sigh of relief. The corpse had disturbed him far more than he realized.

Thinking back to the early years of the apocalypse, Bill recalled rumors that the virus was created in a lab, and that the dead could potentially stay reanimated for decades, the virus keeping the corpse alive far beyond all reason. "Kinda proved that, didn't ya?" he asked the decomposing woman.

With the zombie dead, and the rest of the apartment clear, Bill took his time looting the rooms. Bottle of pills and feminine articles in the bathroom, several cans of food, a case of bottled water, and other various items he found useful went into pillowcases and cloth grocery bags. These he piled next to the door before leaving.

The three remaining apartments above the coffee shop were of a similar layout, and he went through them quickly, relieved to find each empty of once-human inhabitants.

The second apartment yielded the biggest surprise. In a cabinet filled with various organic spices and other cooking items, Bill found three cans of green coffee beans, two of which were still sealed.

"Oh hell yes!" He exclaimed louder than intended. "Oh, come to me you beautiful things," he said as he lifted a can in each hand, examining the peeling labels. The canned beans, intended for personal roasting and extended shelf life were once hoarded by preppers and coffee-snobs alike.

The other find was a dresser filled with various sex toys, vibrators, padded handcuffs along with several large boxes of condoms, bottles of lubricant, and batteries. "Damned if it isn't my lucky day." Bill chuckled gleefully as he stuffed the condoms, several bottles of lube and the batteries into his pack. "Bet Janet will pay pretty damn nicely for these."

Clearing the last apartment, Bill sat on the leather sofa in the living area, resting his head for a moment, thinking aloud. "Tons of good shit in here, like they were never looted at all. The downstairs is trashed, but maybe no one came up here. Wonder if all the apartments along here are like this?"

Lifting his head from the dusty couch his eyes grew wide, "I might not have to go deep into the city at all. If there's this much shit in just these four apartments, it could take me months to empty out this one row."

Laughing, Bill kicked his feet, pounding clouds of dust up from the leather. "Hell yeah!"

Getting up from the couch, he looked out a window. "Only a couple hours of daylight left, and I want to check out that gun store before heading back to the car."

Looking around the apartment Bill saw several of the scented candles in jars. "Well, I'd have light." He checked the lock on the door. "Lock's good too. Might as well hole up in here for the night, check the gun shop tomorrow morning, then head back." Nodding to himself, Bill prepared to spend the night locked down.

Speaking to the empty room, Bill said, "Might as well fix up something to eat." Digging through his bag, he pulled out a small backpacker's stove, which he placed on the range-top in the kitchen. Catching the faint scent of smoke, Bill crossed over the hall to the apartment looking out across the street.

The salon was burning brightly inside, flames licking through shattered windows, tasting the dead that had gathered to roast themselves. Runners sprinted into the flames, shamblers shuffled onward, as did the funkers and huskers, which caught fire with a whoosh that Bill could hear through the window.

"Guess that's one way to kill a few at a time." Bill made his way back to the other apartment, unconcerned with the fire raging across the wide street. "It'll burn out, or it won't, not much you can do, Billy-boy."

Preparing his meal, Bill stared at the cans of coffee beans. "Yeah, I think I deserve some coffee, for damn sure."

"Not a chance, Alan. Business is on hold until we get this mess sorted out."

"Oh come on Janet, shit. Ain't nobody knows when something'll go down, I just want half an hour."

"These girls need to be on guard, not on their backs. You come back and talk to me after this shit is settled and well work something out."

"Damn it, Janet, just ten minutes then? How about that?"

Bibi stood up from where she had been resting her elbows on the counter. Narrowing her eyes she glared at the man begging her for some girlie-time. "I'm not gonna say no again, Alan. Next time I'm just gonna smack you across your stupid fuckin' face. No girls, not right now, and you keep your shit up I'll ban your ass from here, and I happen to know that you've pissed Filler off enough that he won't even let you near his girls."

Alan shoulders slumped, his long, greasy hair dangling in his face. He opened his mouth to smart off, give Janet what for, and thought better of it. Turning away without a word, Alan left through the front door, stepping aside to let Doc Shoup through.

"That fella sure looks downhearted."

"Business is on hold until we get things sorted out and tended to, Doc, and he's not happy about it. He'll get over it though. Something I can do for you?"

Doc shuffled his feet, toeing a spot on the floor. "Well, I was wondering if you happened to have any .357 ammunition."

Bibi shook her head. "Sorry Doc, I don't. I'm sure Filler has some, though."

Shrugging, Doc said, "Yeah, I know he does, but I thought I'd buy it from you instead."

"You can afford it, Doc."

Nodding, he said, "Yep, I can, but well… never mind. Thanks anyway, Janet."

Doc Shoup turned away, heading for the door.

"Hey Doc, let me ask you something."

Stopping with his hand on the door-handle, he faced Bibi.

"I'm curious. What's your take on all this?"

"Take? No real take on it, Janet. It's damn ridiculous that humans fight other humans for life when there's plenty of bad shit out there just waiting to munch on folks. Always been unsavory types, always will be. Just a damn stupid shame is all."

Bibi nodded, fully understanding Doc's thoughts. "Doc, you've always done right by me and my girls. If Filler doesn't have that ammo, or he wants to put you in the "owe" column, just come on back here, I may have something stashed away you can use instead."

Doc Shoup pursed his lips, nodding again. "Thanks, Janet. Sure do appreciate that." He pulled the door open, ready to step out.

"You can call me 'Bibi' you know."

Doc chuckled, "Janet works just fine for me." Smiling, Doc let the door shut behind him, making his way across the blacktop toward Filler's.

Bibi shook her head at the closed door,

laughing to herself. "You're an odd duck, Doc."

Returning to her counter, she reached below and took up one of the three pistols sitting there and her cleaning kit, returning to the cleaning she had been doing before Alan the ass had interrupted her.

Ammo may be limited, but she would make sure each gun was ready if needed.

11

Having waited until the following morning for the coffee, Bill stood next to the range-top, where he had set up the tiny backpackers stove. On top of that rested a small non-stick skillet. Salivating at the aromas rising from the roasting coffee beans he shuffled excitedly in place, a child at Christmas in front of a tree stuffed with brightly colored gifts.

The beans popped loudly in the pan. "Number two," he said. "A little longer, just a bit, good and dark." Smoke began to rise, the heavy, bitter aroma of the beans filling the room and bringing back memories of sitting in ridiculously priced coffee shops with directors or fellow actors discussing the next film or an upcoming awards ceremony.

Bill removed the pan, placing it on an iron trivet that had been on the range-top. Extinguishing the fuel canister, he left the tiny folding stove in place to cool.

Unsurprisingly he had found both a French coffee press and a stone mortar and pestle in the same apartment where he had found the canned coffee beans.

The wait for the beans to cool was almost too much to bear, his thoughts circling around that first hot cup.

Using the mortar and pestle, Bill set to grinding the beans into an oily powder while the water came to a boil.

Bill's eyes rolled back into his head at the aroma coming from the press as the coffee steeped for a minute. "Oh, good Lord, yes."

Taking a dusty cup from a cabinet, he wiped it clean and poured his first cup of real coffee in years.

A deep sigh escaped him, almost sounding part sob. The rich, dark brew sent shockwaves of delight bouncing from taste buds to his brain.

"Yes... just yes."

Taking the cup to the couch, he sat and sipped, forgetting for a moment that the world outside these walls, beyond this liquid heaven in his cup was a world of the dead and dying, both fighting for every meal.

By the time the first cup was empty he could feel the caffeine hit his system. Half-remembered drug-fueled parties in Hollywood Hills came to mind. Nothing he had ever taken had felt as divine the drug chasing through his veins at that very moment.

"Not gonna waste a drop," he said, filling the cup with the last of the still-steaming coffee, savoring every sip.

Sighing again, he practically threw himself off the couch. "Time to get busy, Billy-boy. You gotta a lot to do today, and you've got the fuel to do it."

Stowing his pack inside a closet, planning to return here and spend the night, Bill stuffed his pockets with the things he thought he might need like the tiny flashlight, lighter, some jerky, and a bottle of water.

Crossing the hall, he checked on the salon. Though it had burned itself out sometime in the night it still smoldered, tendrils of smoke drifting up to be torn away by the breeze. Corpses of burned and partially melted zombies lay scattered around the building.

He was relieved to see that there were very few shambling around the area.

"Gun shop first, then make your way back, check every damn place along this side," he said, heading for the stairs.

Down in the coffee shop he dispatched a lone shuffler and made his way outside, hoping none of the dead between the gun shop almost three blocks away and where he stood were runners.

Knife in his left hand, right hand resting on the pistol in its drop-leg holster, Bill stepped out onto the sidewalk. Skirting two still-smoking corpses, he moved with speed toward the far end of the block, spiking the first zombie he came to before it knew he was behind it.

Several shufflers wandered the wide intersection bisecting the first and second blocks. Just beyond them, nearly at the far end of the second block, a knot of what looked to Bill to be five or six zombies huddled around something in the street.

Realizing that he was standing in place he muttered, "Don't stop moving, dumbass."

He speed-walked across the intersection, grateful that so far all the dead out on the street were of the slower variety. Avoiding the slower zombies, taking the time to spike only those that were directly in his path, Bill made it to all the way to the next intersection before the milling group of dead spotted him.

One of them opened its mouth, a low rattle passing through shredded lips. Bill watched, still walking, as two of the group began to move in his direction. "Shit, just keep going."

He could see the sign for the gun store jutting from the front of the building at the far end of the next block. Thankfully, that block was clear of any dead.

Bill tossed a glance over his shoulder, checking on the group he had left behind. All five of the zombies now shuffled in his direction, bumping into each other, intent only on the victim.

"Screw you," Bill said quietly, as he crossed the next intersection, moving onto the third block.

With this section clear of zombies, and those behind him moving slowly, Bill began to run, heading straight for the door below the sign. He couldn't help but chuckle at the shop's name, even as he ran. Bunker Bill's Guns and Ammo.

Bill drew deep breaths, his booted feet pounding heavily at the sidewalk. "Almost there, almost there," he muttered.

Still several yards away from the door, Bill's heart nearly stopped its quick beat when another crowd of dead rounded the corner, charging directly toward him.

He processed several facts rapidly. He couldn't turn back into the group of dead following him and he had no time for hesitation. There was no way he could outpace the sprinting horde.

Several vehicles were parked along the curb, two cars and a delivery van, which sat directly in front of Bunker Bill's. Without slowing his stride

Bill leapt up onto the trunk of the first car, over the roof, onto the hood, to the next car and over it.

The runners were now to the second car and surrounding the van. "Twenty of you shits, maybe. Damn it!"

Still moving, Bill's foot barely touched the dusty, slick hood of the van as he vaulted to its higher roof.

"How fuckin' many of you are there?" Bill muttered as he looked down on the horde now scrabbling at the side of the van, trying to reach the meat that was out of reach. He knew there had to be twenty or more. Getting to the door of the gun store was impossible.

He could see that all of the glass was broken, but the bars on the door and windows of the shop had not been breached. "Well, that's something. If the door's locked I may be in luck." Looking around he said, "If you assbags don't eat me first. Fuck! How the hell am I getting…"

A breeze caused the sign above the door to swing slowly back and forth on rings mounted to a thick steel bar. The sign's mount was bolted into the wall. "Oh, what the hell."

Backing to the edge of the van, gaining an extra step, Bill took two strides and launched himself toward the sign. Hands reaching, fingers circling the cold iron, he swung and slammed into the sign itself, it swung out and back, smacking into his chest.

Bill grunted, squeezing the bar tightly to keep from losing his grip. Hands grabbed at his ankles, squeezing, trying to pull him down.

He refused to look.

Biceps flexed, and Bill lifted himself upward, fighting the pulling hands. He pushed up, resting his chest across the bar. Unable to take a full breath, he knew he had to move.

The brick of the building was less than a foot away, and the edge of the roof was four feet up from the sign.

Bill slid sideways along the bar, getting as close to the wall as possible. Then the sign jerked and he could see the bolts pulling out of the wall. He was about to be dumped directly into the middle of the horde.

Terror reared its head full of gnashing teeth, spurring Bill to move with speed. He lifted a leg, getting a knee up on top of the narrow bar. Pushing up, one hand balancing, reaching for the roofline with the other, Bill felt the sign jerk again. "Shit shit shit…"

"No time, dumbass, get up there or fucking die," he chided himself.

Sliding his knee along the bar, closer to the mounting bolts he pushed, rising up and placing the toe of his other boot against the wall.

Less than a foot remained between his fingers and the roof.

Bill hunched his body tightly, wished he could take a breath, and threw himself upward. The mounting bolts crunched as they pulled out, the sign dropping out from underneath him just as his fingers caught the edge.

Bill threw his other hand up, latching on, hanging by fingers alone. Below him the sign crashed into the bars on the door and bounced off, plowing into the crowd of dead, bowling several over, crushing one of them.

Pulling himself up by inches, Bill got an arm over the edge of the flat roof and pushed. One long minute later, exhausted and soaked in sweat, Bill rolled over the edge of the roof and lay still, sucking air and waiting for the finger cramps and the burning sensation in his arms to subside.

Raising only his head, he could see the roof was clear, except for the air-conditioning unit. "Better be a service hatch."

Standing on legs that were still shaky from the adrenaline rush, Bill made his way to the large roof-mounted air-conditioner. Walking around it he found a raised stainless-steel service hatch on the back side of the unit.

"Now for the fun part." Bill new the hatch would be locked from the inside. Crossing mental fingers, he grasped the edge of the hatch with aching hands and pulled.

The hatch lifted a half an inch before catching. Bill continued to pull, grunting with the effort. He could feel the hatch cover flex in his fingers, just enough to give him hope. He released it with a clang and crouched, resting, his already sore fingers stinging from the effort.

After several minutes he stood up, muttering, "Ok you bitch, let's try this again."

It took him three more back-wrenching, finger splitting tries before the hatch finally popped open, throwing him to the rooftop with a thump.

Up, on his knees, Bill stared down a slanted ladder into a dimly illuminated room, directly into the face of one plain-old zombie and one funker, its face drawn and hanging and wobbling like a turkey's wattle.

12

Trina caught Thomas with one of her last glue sticks, using it to paint long tacky smears on the wall.

"Oh good grief, Thomas! Give me that!" She snatched the stick from his hand and he started crying like she had kicked him.

"You hush, Thomas, or I'll have a talk with your momma and Miss Janet about how you've been behaving." The boy instantly went quiet and hung his head, staring at the tiled floor.

"That's what I thought."

With half her normal class size she only had seven kids, from infant to eleven years old. The break from a full group was nice, though the circumstances sucked. Many of their parents simply didn't want their kids too far away should Junction be attacked.

Trina went back to packing up a box of items to take down into Filler's safe room, so that the children would have something to occupy them, keep their mind from whatever horrors may be raging above if they had to hole up in there.

Today she was spending more time baby-sitting and packing up than she was trying to teach anything. The children could feel the tension that had settled over Junction like a wet wool blanket and they were responding with inattentiveness, anger and crying jags for no reason. Teaching was the last thing she could do.

Days like today were the ones that made her question ever making the deal with Janet to take over the day-care and education of Junction's youth, especially those children born of Janet's "employees".

She received little in compensation from the parents, but Janet made sure she had food and water, and she was allowed to live in the building she used as her school. The other plus was that she didn't have to work on her back, unless she wanted something extra, then she just had to let Janet know that she was on the market for a night or two.

As Trina placed a tattered grade school textbook into the box she heard the door open and turned expecting to see a parent of one of the children.

"Oh, hiya there Earl, what's up?"

"Trina, Filler asked me to come see when you'd have that stuff ready to take down into the basement."

"Just finishing up now Earl, I've got two boxes of stuff. Would you mind taking them over for me? I can't leave the kids alone."

Earl glared at her for a moment, about to ask if she thought he was some sort of bitch-boy. He reconsidered, knowing that to be on the bad side of both Filler and Janet at the same time was just asking for a whole new level of shit-on-a-stick.

"I'll take one and send somebody over for the other, girl."

She could feel the contempt he felt for her and all the other working girls as if he were an old-fashioned radiator and the boiler was kicked up on high.

"Thank you, Earl," she said, flashing him a big, toothy grin. "You really are just a sweetheart, aren't you?" She could see it rankled the old prude to hear her speak so sweetly right to his face, and she reveled in it.

Earl grunted, twisting his mouth up in disgust. Without another word, Earl picked up one of the boxes Trina indicated and headed for the door. He pressed his back to the door and shoved it open, tossing one last glaring look at Trina as he went.

"Whatever, you old grump," she grumbled at the closed door.

The cry of a child snapped her back to the moment. Thomas and Andy had taken little Tina's hand stitched rag doll and were tossing it back and forth, giggling as the girl hopped back and forth between the boys trying to catch the flying cuddle.

"Boys, you give that back right now!"

Both dropped their arms, the doll slapping softly against Andy's chest and falling to the floor. She saw the look the boys shared, a faint grin passing between them. Trina rolled her eyes, knowing that she would be scolding them again within ten minutes for some new mischief they cooked up in those devious little brains.

"Zombies might be easier to corral and keep calm," she whispered to herself.

13

Bill knelt at the opening, sweat dripping from his forehead to splash on the upturned faces of the dead men hungrily staring back at him. "No going back, Billy-boy. This is the reason you came here."

He didn't know what to expect once inside the gun shop, but he hoped and prayed that it had somehow survived any looting that had happened in the area. A stock of weapons and ammo would certainly set him up in comfort.

"Nothin's easy anymore, that's for damn sure. Hell, an easy life now just means you don't worry about getting eaten every minute of the day, doesn't it? If I get a good load going, maybe employ some of the other scavs from Junction to make big hauls out of here I might even try to buy out Phil. Set up some better defenses. Maybe even expand Junction. Now that's a damn good idea, Billy-boy."

Bill realized he was delaying the inevitable. Hovering over the hole, he drew the holstered pistol and pressed the button to drop the magazine, intending to check his ammo, though he was certain he had one in the chamber and two left in the mag.

Drop the magazine he did. It slipped through sore, blood-slicked fingers and down into the open mouth of the funker with a sucking noise. Even in the dim light he could see the bottom of the magazine peeking up at him from that rotting flesh-hole.

The funker didn't seem to notice.

"Are you fucking KIDDING ME!"

His shoulders slumped, hanging his head and sighing, Bill wanted to cry or beat something or fall asleep and wake up in happy land. He had only been awake for a few hours, but the excitement and adrenaline had burned off the energizing effects of the coffee. Now, exhaustion and emotion threatened to put him under.

Bill looked at the pistol stupidly for a moment before checking to be sure that there actually was a round in the chamber. "Fuck it." He slammed in his empty back-up magazine, sighted down on the face of the shuffler and squeezed.

Zombie brains splattered the funker as its partner's head was cored through with the heavy .40 caliber ball. It did not seem to notice that the shuffler had fallen. The sound of the shot spurred it into increased activity, attempting to scale the ladder. The obscene swish and swing of the facial skin sagging almost to its chest made Bill's stomach roll.

Bill thumbed the slide release, sending the bolt home on an empty chamber. He jammed the pistol back into place and fixed the strap over it before reaching for his knife.

"Son-of-a-bitch!" he swore when it dawned on him that he had lost it in his mad leap and climb to the roof. The only weapon he had left was the heavy gauntlet. "It'll have to do," he said with a shrug.

"Here I come, asshole." Bill went through the hole, and stepped down the canted ladder backward, his shoulders resting against the steps. When he was one rung above the grasping hands of the nasty dead thing he paused. He knew that if he stopped to think he would balk, and possibly screw up, get himself killed, so he jumped.

He went out, over the left shoulder of the funker, turning in midair, as the zombie twisted around, arms reaching up. As he came down he swung his arm in a wide arc, using both muscle and gravity to bring the gauntlet down dead center on the funker's head with force.

The skull split and shattered with a wet crack. Rotting brain tissue splattered out to both sides. Bill saw it as if watching a movie, in slow motion, the gore splashing out in a wave on either side of the head, both eyeballs popping free, one tearing away completely and smacking him in the chest with a liquid splat, the other bobbing at the end of its nerve tether.

Bill failed to stick the landing.

His feet slid the moment he hit the ground. With his gauntlet buried deeply in the skull he pulled the fully-dead funker down on top of him as he fell. Bill cried out in pain as his tailbone met concrete and the funker landed square on his chest, knocking the air from him.

He was able to guide the funker's head with the gauntleted arm, preventing a mouth to mouth encounter.

Trying to suck air through lungs already compressed by the weight of the dead zombie was nearly impossible, and a moment of true terror swelled in Bill as he felt the darkness at the edges of his vision spreading out. Don't pass out, don't pass out... became an instant litany in his mind.

Levering with the gauntlet arm, pushing with his right hand, and rolling his body, he was able to shift the funker off and to the floor, though the gauntlet was still firmly lodged in the thing's head.

Lying next to the foul smelling dead thing and trying to draw air into lungs that felt paralyzed would shatter the mind of most.

With his first full breath Bill laughed, at the zombies, at his lodged gauntlet, at his own terror, at the cloying reek of the funker. Then he vomited.

If not for the reeking dead and his own vomit right next to his head, he would have lain there on the floor for several more minutes collecting himself, reassembling the pieces of his mind that decided to head for the hills for the duration of the scary shit, but the smells of puke and funker were powerful motivators.

Bill rolled onto his side and pushed up, lifting the zombie head several inches from the ground. Getting fully to his feet, he placed a boot against the funker's head and pulled.

The gauntlet came free with a squishing pop and Bill stumbled backward but kept his feet beneath him. Walking back to the dead funker, Bill slipped two fingers into the zombie's mouth, shuddering when his knuckles brushed cold, slimy, dead lips. He pulled the magazine from its throat, flicking it, flinging large drops of fleshy gore onto the floor before dropping it into an empty pocket. He would clean it later. Ammo was far too precious to leave behind.

He could see that he was in a small back room, storage for basic supplies like toilet paper and cleaning materials.

He walked through the open door leading toward the shop area, passing through another storage room, this one made up of mostly a heavy wire cage. The lock that had held it closed had been battered to pieces.

"Yeah, figures," he said, hoarsely. The gun shop had been looted.

After everything he had done to get in here, Bill wasn't about to leave Bunker Bill's Guns and Ammo without giving it a full once over. "Eh, hell, maybe something was left behind."

Bill scanned the shop-front, eyes following the long L-shaped counter, and the empty gun racks and smashed glass display cases. Out on the floor, t-shirt and hat displays had been knocked to the ground. Piles of unwanted items, like the clothes, reloading set-ups, branded merchandise, and other outdoors odds and ends like camping equipment were scattered over the sales floor.

It appeared that the looters had been more destructive than efficient, taking guns and ammunition and smashing through everything else.

Kicking his way through the trash, Bill showed no concern over the knot of zombies now pressing against the bars of the doors and windows, hands out and grasping at the air.

"Oh yeah, there's plenty of good shit left in this mess." Feeling dejected at the lack of guns and ammo in the guns and ammo store, he took a moment to lean over an unbroken section of the counter, hanging his head and squeezing the back of his neck to relieve the tension that had built up since he left the apartment this morning.

Frustrated, he knocked an empty display off the counter. It flew back against the vacant gun racks, and slammed to the floor. An almost musical tinkling, skittering noise came from the floor behind the sales counter.

Pulling himself over to look, Bill smiled in surprise. The floor was littered with loose rounds, from shotgun shells to various calibers of brass ammo.

"Well holy crap."

The only thing he could think was that in their haste, the looters had dropped and trampled boxes of bullets. Instead of taking the time to scoop up the fallen ammo they left it, absconding with whatever they had in hand.

He walked around the counter, careful not to step on anything. It was obvious from the discoloration of some of the brass that it had been laying here for a long time, but it he was confident that some of it was still viable.

Kicking through the mess on the store floor, Bill found a tipped shelf hiding a pile of plastic ammo boxes. He took several to the unbroken counter and began scooping the loose ammunition up with a dustpan.

It took him just over thirty minutes to sweep it all up. He had filled five and about a third of a sixth box by the time he dumped the last scoop. Picking through the boxes, Bill looked at the base of round after round until he had set twenty-five identical bullets out on the counter-top. Bill chambered a round, loading one more into the magazine, for a total of thirteen in the gun.

He grabbed a shirt and a small bottle of gun oil from the floor. He dismantled the magazine that had been lodged in the funker's mouth, wiped it clean, and oiled the entire thing before loading it to capacity as well.

"A thousand rounds of ammo is more than anyone has seen at one time in years. Even Filler, who has a tidy little stockpile of ammo," he told the empty store. "Damn shame there wasn't more, and some guns to go with it."

Scouring the whirlwind mess of the sales floor, Bill found several small bubble-packed flashlights, batteries included. He cracked one open, inserted the batteries, and thumbed the button.

"Hot damn!" he said when the light came on, brilliant in the dim room. "Now that's cake!" He was unable to stifle the wide grin spreading across his face.

He shined the light across the zombie horde still pressing against the security bars. Several of the dead were caught between the iron bars, their heads having been squeezed through by the crush of the others. Bill shook his head. "Have to do something about you bastards before I can get out of here, won't I?"

Shooting them was out of the question. He didn't want to draw in more and conserving his new-found ammo for times when it would be truly necessary was a top priority.

Next to a mound of fishing equipment, Bill found what he considered ideal for his need. He took a moment to open the packaging and assemble the telescoping rod. He then mounted the four-prong trident of the frog gig and planted it on the floor next to his foot like a warrior on the battlefield. With the rod fully extended and locked into place he had a twelve-foot long spear.

With a gleeful cackle, Bill moved toward the front of the shop and the horde waiting there.

Working in a rhythm of jab, twist, yank, he was able to spike every dead thing outside the windows within thirty minutes. His arms shook from the effort. The day's activities had taken their toll and it was just now going on noon. "I need a fuckin' nap," Bill Robb muttered.

Bill walked toward the back room, propping the frog gig on the shattered counter as he passed by. Taking out his new flashlight, he explored the back rooms, finding nothing of any real importance, other than a case of toilet paper. It wasn't heavy, but it's bulky size would make it hard to carry out. "Few rolls at a time. Fuck, maybe I won't tell the others about this. A lot of good shit I can trade, set myself up a nice place in the walls of Junction."

Scaving was always a lot of risk, with little chance of reward. A few cans of goods well past their expiration, or clothing that wasn't rotted and falling apart. Things like guns and ammunition, toilet paper, batteries, those things that held the most value were rare, and often in such deplorable condition that they were beyond useless.

Though there were no guns, and he certain that much of the loose ammunition he found would be too corroded to fire, the gun shop still held many items of value. The flashlights and batteries alone would be enough to put him in good stead with every trader in Junction for months. The camping and fishing gear, hiking equipment, knives and sharpening stones, even the several cases of emergency food bars, which were only a couple of years past their use-date, were of great value to a world that had nearly forgotten what having these things truly meant.

In the back room, inside the looted storage cage, Bill stretched out on the heavy rubber mats that covered the floor and rested.

14

Bill raised his head, feeling groggy and disoriented. He wasn't sure how long he had slept on the rubber mat, but he could tell that the light coming through the door from the front of the shop was dusky. "Well this could be a long night if you don't get up and get out of here."

Bill rubbed the sleep from his eyes and scrubbed his face with dry hands to wake himself fully. "Well, let's make this happen, Billy-boy." Slapping the hard rubber mat, and leaning forward, still trying to convince himself to move, Bill heard a noise through the uncomfortable stillness. Cocking his head sideways, he listened intently.

The sound was muffled, almost buried beneath the sound of the blood rushing through his ears. A soft wet noise, like the gently moving waves at the edge of a wind-swept pond.

"What the hell?"

The sound stopped, leaving Bill to wonder if he had even heard it. He stared down at the black shoe-scuffed rubber and thought. Raising his hand he slapped the mat again and listened.

The sound came again, wet and sloshing, possibly from beneath him. "Well, ok then."

On hands and knees, Bill Robb crawled the mat until he found a seam. He picked at it for a moment with sore fingers before flipping open a pocket knife he had rescued from the mess out front and liberated from its bubble packaging.

Digging the clip-point into the seam he pried, lifting the edge of the mat. Slipping the blade in even further he was able to get the mat up far enough to slip his hand under the cool rubber and lift. The mat pulled back to reveal a solid concrete floor.

"Hmmph, ok then." He inched over to try another section.

Minutes later Bill had pulled up and peeled back a large flap of the floor-covering to reveal another section of concrete similar to the last, except for the metal hatch hidden toward the back corner of the cage.

"Well holy shit! Bunker Bill had a bunker!"

Bill Robb's heart began to pound with excitement and anticipation of what might be below the hatch. "Damn sure some water down there, and something moving around in it. You down there waiting for some company, Bunker Bill?" He asked the hatch.

Bill knelt down and lifted a wide pull handle that folded down flush into the top of the hatch. It refused to budge, no matter how hard he pulled.

Bill paced in front of the hole in the floor that refused him entry. "Think, Bill, think." He knew he had seen similar hatches and doors and racked his brain to draw the memories up from the dark well where they were hidden.

"Ok, so the hatch looks pretty simple, but uh, if it's one of those that locks closed with a wheel there's no way you're getting' it open, short of having a pound or two of explosives. If it's a single point lock, then prying it might work. Back breaking, but it might. Fuck it, I'm getting' in there."

Bill was determined, his heart set on whatever was inside that bunker. He wandered through the piles and scattered mess of the front of the store, kicking debris and loot aside, looking for something to use as a pry bar.

Under one pile his boot struck something that clanked against the tile floor. Under a mound of clothes and rotted boxes he found a crowbar. "Hot damn, now that's cake!" He hefted the bar, noticing how light it was compared to the usual crowbar. Looking closely he saw the word TITANIUM stamped in the haft. "Ok, now we're in business," he said with a grin.

Returning to the storage cage and the waiting hatch, Bill swigged the last drops from his bottle of water and tossed the empty aside.

With determined gusto, he set the tip of the bar in the thin crack between the hatch and the edge of the steel inset and began his work.

****

Three hours and several scraped knuckles later, just as he was on the verge of giving up, the hatch gave a low grating noise and lifted an inch, before stopping. "Oh hell yeah, I've got you now, you stubborn bitch!"

Bill worked by flashlight, pressing the crowbar further into the crack, leaning all his weight on it. Over his grunting and cursing he could hear the almost constant swish and splash of water below.

"I'm comin' Bunker Bill, just hang on a bit more," he wheezed. "Give you a rest and see what you got down there."

With a heave and groan, Bill Robb shoved

hard on the crowbar and was rewarded with another grinding noise from the hatch. The hatch popped, lifting several inches and Bill stumbled to the side, lost his balance and plopped to the floor, exhausted.

The splashing was louder now, and he crawled to the hatch, pushing it until it flopped back, catching on rods inside that kept it in an upright position.

Bill shined his light down through the hole, into the rotted face of a man he assumed to be Bunker Bill. "Hello there Bill, I'm Bill. You might remember me from the movies, back in the day."

The zombie moaned softly in reply.

"Yeah, I know. This scar does make it a bit difficult to recognize me," he said, running a finger over the thick puckering on his cheek. "Well Bill, give me a second to catch my breath and I'll come down and pay you a visit."

Zombie Bill stared up at living Bill, oblivious to the light shining in his face, only hearing the noise. "Alrighty then, Billy-boy. Get your head on straight and let's do this thing."

He stood in front of the hole holding the crowbar, the hooked end dangling toward his feet. Without another word he turned and lowered himself down the ladder.

15

Bibi sat in the single chair she kept in her room. Stuffing leaked out of holes, and the cushion was covered in strips of duct-tape. It was ugly, like much of the cobbled together life inside the walls of Junction. Also like Junction, the chair was somewhat comfortable and served its purpose well.

In her lap was the mangiest looking cat anyone had seen in years. It was also just about the only cat anyone had seen in years. Bibi stroked the thin, shedding fur of the animals back, losing herself in the cat's deep purring and the comfort the small warm creature offered.

"You're a good cat aren't you, Fuggs?" She cooed to the sleepy cat.

The cat, which she had named Fugly, was a creature of the zombie wastelands, torn and ragged and untrusting of all but Bibi. With an ear half torn off, one eye missing, a fang and several teeth that showed through a tear in its lower lip, and the crooked bend of the tail, the cat appeared the epitome of a feline nightmare. It was also just as mean as it looked.

She had tried to keep Fugly out at the check in counter with her or let him follow her whenever she went for walks or to check on her girls, but far too many had been scratched or bitten, and far too many had threatened to capture and cook the cat, so she left the angry creature in her room. He didn't seem to mind.

"In a world where zombies crawl the earth," she said in a mock movie announcer voice, "men are still dipshits."

Laughing at her own joke, she stood, cradling Fugly close to her bosom for a moment before placing him back in the chair.

From the mini-fridge that was now just a dead thing to store her water in, she took a plastic bottle, wrinkled and warped from multiple re-uses. Taking a hefty swig, draining it, she sat the empty aside and said to the still sleeping cat, "Gonna have to see about the water purification, it's been tasting funny lately." Fugly's crooked tail twitched.

Fugly jumped up in the chair, back arching when a knock came at the door. "Calm down, Fuggs, I got it."

Opening the door as far as the security catch would allow she peered through the narrow gap.

Outside her door, shifting foot to foot was Marian, a dour look on her face.

"Can I talk to you for a minute, Janet?"

"One second." Bibi closed the door, flipped the security catch back, re-opened the door and stepped outside. "Can't have Fugly out here, he's likely to climb up you and scratch your face just for the hell of. What's up, Marian?"

Tears wavered in Marian's eyes. "Maybe I should just go, find Mitchell's group, tell them I killed him. I can't stand the thought that there're people here who are going to get hurt, maybe even die because of me."

Bibi thought for a moment before responding. "Well, I have to tell you, I appreciate your guts. But Junction is on those boy's radar now, and they sure as hell aren't going to just turn around and walk away from what they think will be easy pickins just because you offered yourself up. We're all in this now." Looking deep into the terrified woman's eyes, she said, "To tell you the truth, I'm surprised we haven't been hit by them before. We've dealt with all kinds of mess around here, girl, from a zombie horde over a thousand strong to various bastardly individuals. It may not look like it, but Junction can hold her own."

Marian looked back, Janet's words sinking in. After a moment she nodded. "Ok, well, is there anything I can do, then?"

"Seems you done got your courage up. Get yourself a weapon and be ready for whatever comes along. If you have to see Filler about a gun, let me know, I'll help you square it up with him shortly after this whole damn thing is done."

"Yes, ma'am."

Bibi reached out, resting her hand on Marian's arm. "This is your home now, girl, we got your back, and you get ours. We have our own little issues around here, power struggles and politicking, but the folks around here are mostly decent, hard, mean, half-crazy, but decent. None should be fucked with, not a one, but they're good folks, most of 'em."

Marian nodded, wiping a tear from beneath her eye. "Thanks, Janet."

"Any time, Marian. Get yourself squared away, and sweetheart, you keep that courage."

Bibi watched as the girl nodded again and walked away. "You got this, girl," she said under her breath. Back inside the room, Bibi scooped up her mangy, angry cat and cuddled with him in the chair once more.

You took the small joys when you could get them, because who knew what the next hour or day might bring.

16

The Vespa sputtered and buzzed and whined as Corey drove slowly down the buckled blacktop of the narrow county road. He knew that eventually it would die, leaving him stranded in place, he only hoped he was close to some safe haven when it happened.

Fuel was precious, as was keeping the scooter alive, but Corey was wasting time now, avoiding Junction for as long as he could, giving the people there a little more time to find something else to fret over other than Laidlaw and what he had done.

Tooling down the back roads, enjoying the emptiness of it all, Corey's mind plotted and planned. His goal was to eventually be what Filler was to Junction, the main man, the one everyone feared and respected all at once.

Part of that was removing his competition, or anyone he thought might slow down the progress of moving that plan forward. Anyone, like Laidlaw, who Corey knew would hold back the others in Junction from lifting him up, praising his ingenuity, resourcefulness, ability to provide and protect. And rule.

Tall weeds along the roadside whipped by, casting the buzzing rattle of the scooter back at Corey. In the distance he could see what appeared to be a deer or other animal laying in the weeds, pressing them flat.

"If it's pretty fresh that would be some great meat to take back," he said into the wind. He revved the engine, increasing his speed with his excitement.

As he closed in on the spot, he realized that it wasn't an animal. He should have known. No one had seen a deer in ages.

Then he recognized the bloody jacket. "Frito…"

Corey was nearly right on top of Frito when he saw the man struggle into a sitting position. He could see bloody holes poked through shirt and jacket. The wounds were large and looked to him like spear holes. "Ha, fuckin' Sores got you, didn't they, dumbass," he said into the wind.

Corey stopped the Vespa next to the sitting scav, turning off the key to conserve fuel. He climbed off the scooter and slipped his swimming goggles up to rest on his forehead, making him look like a four-eyed frog.

Frito's swollen face followed Corey as he approached. A wide split just below his right eye still wept thin trickles of blood. The larger wounds had clotted over, the blood dark and tacky at the edges.

"How ya doing, buddy?"

Frito's glazed eyes tried to focus, pain and extreme thirst wrecking his ability to think.

"Water," Frito said, the word distorted from his pasty, thick tongue.

"Sure, buddy," Corey said, his thoughts twisting and quick. "Let's get you on the wagon first. Can you stand?"

Frito was barely able to even shake his head.

"Here, let me help you."

Corey knelt beside Frito and put an arm around him. He pushed with his legs, lifting Frito. Corey began to walk toward the Vespa, Frito's feet dragging more than taking steps.

With his free hand, the one that wasn't holding Frito up, Corey reached down, pulled his knife free and raised it quickly, jamming it deep into Frito's side. He felt the blade jar in his hand as he nicked a rib. He was certain he had punctured a lung.

Frito gasped, his eyes burning bright again from the sudden pain.

Corey withdrew his arm, and Frito collapsed to the pavement. The dripping knife remained in Corey's other hand.

Corey stood above Frito, watching the man bleed. Looking into his eyes, Corey asked Frito, "Do you want to know why?"

Frito's mouth moved, but no sound came forth and Corey smiled as he turned away, mounted the Vespa, started it and drove away without looking back, leaving the question unanswered.

Frito could see a rivulet of blood spreading out, following irregularities in the road. His blood stood out stark and brilliant against the faded, dusty blacktop, sunlight glittering in the lengthening pool.

He stared at a tire track, left when the Vespa had splashed through his blood, until he closed his eyes against the pain.

Both the buzzing of the Vespa and Frito faded until they were gone.

Ripley, Believe it or Not

After leaving Janet's, Frito and Tool went to their separate shacks.

The next morning Frito stopped by Filler's to get a jar of stew and some water. He was leaving on a short run to the west. He knew Corey had gone north on that shitty little Vespa and he didn't want to run into the murderous prick. Laidlaw was an asshole but what Corey did was a bit much even by Junction standards.

Frito left using the south gate. Mitch Burton was on duty and told him that everything looked clear, no movement for miles in any direction. That was good news for Frito who wasn't excited about the possibility of encountering the sprinter zombies that Tool had told him about.

A couple months earlier when returning from a long run, Frito had seen a small town set on the side of a hill near a river. He hoped it was small enough to have been overlooked by other scavengers.

Unlike Tool, Frito preferred not to move at night. He set up his blanket hammock at dusk, ate a little stew with corn chips and slept lightly while listening for the snap of the fishing line trip wire strung out around his camp. As the sun rose, he gathered his gear and continued west. By late afternoon he could see the houses in the distance. Using a battered pair of binoculars he surveyed the area.

The road ran up to a bridge over a muddy river then continued past the little town. One small turn-off wound up the hill and amongst the houses. It would be dark soon, so he decided to get a little closer and set up camp in the trees that lined the east side of the river.

At dusk he saw movement on the winding hill road. There was just enough light for him to make out two dirty Sores walking towards the bridge. They built a fire and sat down on a couple buckets. Light from a second fire could be seen in the windows of one of the houses. Frito figured there must be six or eight Sores holed up in the town. This was going to complicate things, but Frito figured he'd come this far, might as well go all the way.

The people of Junction didn't have many secrets. Eventually, everyone would know your business, your choice of weapons, your skill set, your sexual preferences, how much you owed and to whom. Since coming to Junction, Frito had managed to keep two secrets. First was the location of his corn chip stash. He decided it was time to utilize his second secret.

From his worn ALICE pack he pulled out a small purple bag with the words Crown Royal stitched onto it. Next was a black plastic rifle butt. He pulled off the cap and assembled the AR-7 rifle. It took only a minute to attach the receiver to the stock and then screw on the barrel. Opening the purple bag he removed eight rounds, loaded the magazine, then put one more in the chamber before sliding the magazine home and thumbing the safety to ON.

Frito didn't put a lot of faith in the rifle. Within twenty-five yards it was usually good for a headshot. Beyond twenty-five yards the accuracy dropped considerably. Jams were frequent and required dropping the magazine and working the bolt to clear, if you were lucky. If you weren't lucky, it was necessary to pry the jammed cartridge out with the tip of a knife. While it was light enough to carry, it was too light to serve as a decent club should the need arise. Still, it usually went bang and would give him an edge against the superior numbers he would be up against later tonight.

Frito readied for what he was certain would be a difficult encounter. The rifle was loaded. Knives strapped on in various locations. His prize kukri held a place of honor on the right hip. The heavy blade was capable of cleaving flesh with ease. Three kitchen knives, one in each boot and one on his left side would serve as backups should he need them. Confident with his preparations he sat down against a tree and relaxed for a few hours before making his move.

Creeping up to the edge of the road he knelt at the east end of the bridge using the guard rail as cover. The little peep sight on the AR-7 was near useless in the dark so he waited until one of the guards bent to put more wood on their fire. He judged the distance to be just over twenty yards, the fire backlit his target making it possible for him to place the front sight directly on the guard's temple as he poked at the coals. POP. The Sore fell over onto the fire without making a sound. The second guard stood up in amazement at what he had witnessed, then turned to look in Frito's direction, still not certain what was happening. The tattered clothing of the dead Sore caught fire as a second shot went into the chest of the bewildered guard who screamed out as he fell to ground.

Frito checked the rifle, cleared a jammed shell, added two rounds to the magazine and held his position waiting for the remainder of the Sores to show themselves. As the wounded guard whimpered in pain four shadowy figures moved rapidly down the hill. As they got close to the fire they slowed and took defensive postures, looking in every direction for the attackers. Holding the rifle to his side, Frito rose and moved from behind the guard rail to stand in plain sight. When the Sores saw him they cautiously moved in his direction. So far everything was going as planned.

When they were half way across the bridge, Frito quickly raised the rifle and fired two rounds into the nearest Sore, dropping him. Next, he fired into the largest of the three remaining men. One round struck the man but the AR-7 jammed and Frito dropped it to the ground, opting to unsheathe the kukri rather than fumble with the rifle. The big wounded Sore let out a roar and charged. His left arm was hanging limp, in his right hand was a rusty butcher knife. Just as the man closed, Frito side-stepped and clothes-lined the Sore with the kukri, nearly decapitating him.

The last two Sores were far more cautious. They spread out to either side of the bridge in an effort to flank him. Frito briefly considered retreating, hoping to separate them in the trees but discarded the idea as it would mean leaving the jam-o-matic rifle for them to pick up and possibly use against him. As they circled around, Frito briefly thought that this might be the end until making eye contact with the Sore in front of him. His attacker was having doubts, uncertain that even the two of them could take the stranger with the curved blade. The uncertain Sore made a half-hearted lunge, Frito ignored the weak effort and spun around as the man behind him was coming in fast with an overhand stab. Sidestepping the clumsy attack, Frito swung the kukri in a wide arc that ended at the base of his attacker's skull. The blade stuck fast in the bone. Unable to wrench it free he rolled away and rose to his feet, a kitchen knife clenched firmly in his fist, ready for an attack that never came. The coward ran back across the bridge then turned up the road towards the little town. Frito watched the high-speed shadow disappear into the Sore's house. It would be light in a few hours and Frito saw no reason to pursue the retreating man who no longer posed a threat.

His favorite blade was now clean and back in its sheath. The AR-7, once disassembled, was returned to its place in the bottom of his pack. Frito cautiously crossed the bridge, found the wounded Sore unconscious near the fire, and quickly dispatched him before heading up the hill past a sign that read, "Welcome to Ripley pop. 110", straight to the house the Sores had been using. A steel drum that had served as an indoor fire pit could be seen, still smoking, through the open door. Kukri in hand, Frito entered the house and began a thorough search. Once convinced that the ground floor was vacant he entered the basement through a door in the kitchen. Shelves lined the limestone walls, but all were bare except for a few empty Mason jars.

Fairly certain that the last Sore had hightailed it out of town, Frito searched house after house, finding little of value. A few towels and a couple bedsheets from an undisturbed closet. Three canning jars full of vegetables from the back of a basement shelf. The big score, an entire attic full of clothes including two pair of boots, a stiff canvas jacket, three pair of denim jeans and miscellaneous women's clothing. He filled the duffel bag that had been folded up in his ALICE pack before starting back down the hill towards the bridge.

On the walk back to Junction, Frito decided to break the rules once again. When he was within sight of Junction, he sorted through his recent acquisitions. Some of the women's clothing and one pair of boots were wrapped up in the old jacket before being tied shut. Once through the gate Frito went straight to Doc's, dropped off the jacket bundle without bothering to wake the cantankerous old man, then continued on to Filler's.

As usual he went in the back door, dropped his duffel bag by Filler's office door, grabbed a bowl of stew and found Tool waiting with a pitcher of water.

"Saw you come in, how come I got here first?"

"Where's Maynard?" Frito asked.

Tool took the hint. "Guarding my shack. He's taken to watching after my stuff when he isn't sleeping at Doc's. Pretty sure the old man is feeding him. How'd you do?"

"I'm still alive and there's half a bag of stuff

in the kitchen, so I'd call it a success."

"Zombies?"

"No. Ran into some Sores. They probably cleared out the zoms before I got there. Of course, they cleaned out pretty much everything else too."

"Pretty much?" Tool gave Frito a knowing look.

Frito smiled and gave a quick wink. "What say we have a drink with Doc when I finish eating?"

Tool signaled the kitchen girl. When she got to the table, Tool ordered, "Bowl to go." He slipped her two tampons and a maxi-pad with a nod. The girl returned momentarily and set a plastic jar of stew on the table. From her baggy shirt she eased a bottle which Tool slipped into his jacket as she hurried back to the kitchen.

Frito and Tool entered Doc's just as he was wiping out three glasses. "Figured you boys would be coming around for a drink. That must be your stuff."

"The coat is for you Doc. The rest I got plans for."

"Appreciate that, kid, but you know Filler is going to throw a fit when he finds you been holding out on him."

"No secrets here in Junction, least not for long." Tool chimed in as he poured from the smuggled bottle.

"Yeah, I know. The boots are for Janet. The ladies' clothes are for Trina."

"Trina? You two an item? I gotta get out of this office more often."

"Nothing between Trina and me, Doc. Just thought I'd do something nice for her. She's a decent woman and deserves something for her efforts here."

Doc and Tool nodded agreement as they clinked their glasses.

"Frito, I'm going back out in a couple days, what say we make a run together?"

"Not this time, I'm leaving tomorrow morning. Got to get back there and finish that place off then pick up some more corn chips. Down to my last bag."

"So, no Janet's tonight?" Tool smiled.

The Boys are Back

Frito got to Ripley and went straight to the gold mine attic where he left off on his last trip. There were still some lady's clothes to get, a few miscellaneous items to be had including a small mirror, a little music box, and a bottle of Brut cologne. "Maybe Filler will use this so he doesn't smell like hog shit and sweat." Frito laughed out loud at the thought of Filler dabbing the Brut behind his ears.

Once finished with the attic he continued to search the small town. There was a large grain bin behind a nearby farm house on the outskirts of Ripley. Frito could smell the rat feces when he got close. The rats were not a threat, what bothered him were the cinderblock deadfalls set up in the area. None of them were tripped.

Frito quickly turned and headed for the bridge. Halfway across, he glanced back to see two

Sores following him. When he turned back two more emerged at the opposite end of the bridge. With nowhere to run he would have to make a stand. He dropped the duffel and the ALICE pack. No time to assemble the rifle, he'd have to rely on his Kukri. Curved blade in hand, Frito charged the two filthy men blocking his way.

On the Road Again

He awoke on the side of the road, unsure as to how he had gotten there. Despite the pain, he rose and began to put one foot in front of the other. Left foot, right foot, left foot, right foot. The spear wounds had clotted over but he was finding it more and more difficult to keep moving. Dehydration was taking its toll. Although he had walked all through the night Frito knew that he was still far from seeing the walls of Junction. Unable to go any further he collapsed beside the road. It felt good to lay there in the weeds and he quickly passed out.

The annoying buzz of flies woke him a short time later. Frito wanted to swat at them, but his arms were heavy and unwilling. The buzzing was getting louder. It took all the effort he could gather to get into a sitting position. His vision was blurry, but Frito could see something moving on the road. The incessant buzzing continued to get louder, rising from annoying to ear splitting.

Corey turned off the ratty Vespa, pulled off his swim goggles and greeted Frito. "How ya doing buddy?"

"Water."

"Sure buddy. Let's get you on the wagon first. Can you stand?"

Frito shook his head weakly.

"Here, let me help you."

Corey knelt beside Frito putting an arm around his waist and standing, pulling Frito up with him. As the pair moved slowly onto the road and towards the Vespa there was a sudden shooting pain in Frito's side. Corey let go and as Frito fell to the ground the knife was wrenched from his side. Corey stood there, knife in hand, smiling.

"Do you want to know why?"

It was getting hard to breathe and Frito could see a rivulet of blood streaming across the pavement. He watched as Corey started the Vespa and turned it towards Junction, nearly running him over in the process. As the buzzing faded into the distance Frito gave in to the darkness.

The Guardian's Love

It wasn't an easy decision, but in the end, she felt it was what she needed to do. She only hoped he would still be there in that ugly place. After watching him sleep that first night, she had returned to the dilapidated carnival she called home only to lay awake thinking about him. Thinking about how beautiful he was and how badly she wanted to touch him, to hold him close, just as she had done with her lover so long ago. She knew that this man was not him. She knew that he could not love her back, not in her new form. Still, she had decided to follow him in that ugly little car with that ridiculous toilet on wheels. She had followed him just to get a glimpse of him each time the car stopped. Now she was going back there to find him.

No doubt the filthy people or the dead would destroy her carnival home in her absence, but maybe it was time. She had protected it for so long. And why? Because it reminded her of days long gone? Of a life long gone? Even so, her humanity had been slipping away for some time when the man in the camo jacket appeared and made her remember, made her feel. Yes, it was time to find him. If only to watch him from a distance.

It wasn't only her appearance that had changed when she transformed. Her senses were heightened now, and she seemed to know instinctually when the sun would rise, where to find water, how to move silently. In short, she had become a wild animal, a predator and she was not happy about that. The man in the camo jacket had given her humanity back to her and she wanted more. So, she left home and moved lithely through the countryside toward the ugly, smelly place where she had last seen him disappearing behind a rusty gate.

She arrived at the place and watched from the cover of a small grove of trees until the next day when she saw him in the distance. He was walking this time. Carrying a duffel bag over his shoulder. Mesmerized by him, she had to stop herself from following as he passed through the gate. She'd seen the men with guns standing guard and knew that she was a monster now, not welcome anywhere.

The following morning, the gate opened and there he was again. Beautiful in his worn camo jacket, walking back the way he'd come the previous day. She watched him disappear out of sight then laid down to sleep. Once it was dark she would follow him again. Perhaps she would get to watch him sleep as she had done before.

For three days, he had walked. Each night he would set a trip wire around his camp before hanging a hammock in the trees. Each night she found him and climbed a nearby tree, easily avoiding his alarm system, and looked down at him. Then, just before sunrise she would slink away.

Now, she was afraid of what might happen. Her new love had crossed the bridge and walked up the road to a quaint little town. She wanted to follow him, but she could smell the filthy people. Judging by the stench, the town must be full of them. So, she waited, crouching in the brush, for him to return.

It wasn't long before she saw him nearly galloping down the hill. As he crossed the bridge the filthy people she had been smelling suddenly sprung their trap. From either end of the bridge they emerged and advanced on him. He was terribly outnumbered by the dirty men as he dropped his duffel bag, armed himself, and charged at the ones who blocked his way.

They stopped her love with their crude weapons, sharpened sticks, shards of glass, clubs. Surrounded as he was, he managed to keep them at bay for some time before being knocked to the ground. As the filthy ones closed for the kill, she could stand idle no longer. Leaping from her hiding place she crossed the fifty yards separating her from the man who had made her feel again.

Her new form seemed to have been created for the sole purpose of killing and she proved it beyond a doubt. Rippling muscles tore limbs from bodies, black talons ripped through flesh causing streams of blood to arc out into the air. The filthy men didn't stand a chance against her and when she was finished, they lay in pieces across the blood coated pavement.

She looked then to her love who lay motionless at her feet. Kneeling over him she could hear his heart faintly beating. His warm breath lightly caressing her glossy skin. As gently as her form would allow she lifted him to her breast and carried him away.

For two days, she held him. Periodically carrying his unconscious body to a stream where she did her best to clean his wounds and dribble water from her mouth to his. On the third day, she carried him to the road leading back to his friends. She laid him in the tall grass, briefly touched her black lips to his, then rose to her full height and began to make her way back to Ripley.

Back to the stinking town full of filthy men to exact her revenge.

To Be King in the Land of the Dead – Part 3

1

Bill stood in two inches of cold water that felt slimy sliding across the skin of his ankles as it soaked through is pants and boots. Brackish gore dripped from the crook of the crowbar into the water, splashing softly and making tiny ripples.

Turning in place, Bill's mouth hung open as he gawped at the tiny room filled with various supplies, guns, ammunition, ready-to-eat meals in carton after carton.

Modular shelving lined three of the walls. Along the wall furthest from the ladder a living area had been arranged, with two cots, a cooler, more stacks of food, and case after case of bottled water. A camp stove, rust tracing its edges, sat on top of a metal cabinet. One of the cabinet doors hung open, and inside he could see two-gallon cans of camp fuel pushed next to each other.

Looking down at the carcass that gently bobbed in the shallow water whenever he moved, he whistled and said, "Damn, Bunker Bill, you sure had a layout. You hadn't come down with the sickness you'd have hung on for a helluva long time."

In one of the two cots a body rested, mostly rotted, now more bones than flesh. Slim, tacky threads hung from the underside of the cot where the putrefying tissues had soaked through the heavy canvas.

"Had yourself a roommate, there Bunker

211

Bill? Things went south, and you had a zombie snack, didn't ya?"

Though the smell was ripe and cloying, Bill had smelled far worse odors in just the past two days. The fetor of the dead became a barely noticed tickle at the back of his sinuses within minutes.

Many of guns on the shelves had been left open to the damp that had intruded into the room and were pitted and coated with rust. "Well doesn't that suck," Bill muttered as he wiped at the dust on the barrel of a long rifle.

Though the guns left out were useless, there were many plastic cases lined up on the shelves. He popped the latches on the nearest and whistled at the sight inside. The two guns inside the padded case had rounded edges and handles, and they were short, about as long as his arm. They bore a few small spots of surface rust, but no deep pitting like unboxed guns. "Well what do we have here?" Lifting one of the guns from the padding he held it, felt the contours. The gun was built differently from most of the weapons he had handled. The magazine lay on top of the gun, parallel with it.

Flipping the short weapon over he found a name and number stamped into the side. Fabrique Nationale PS90. "Nice. Have to mess with you, figure out how you work."

Sitting next to the case he found several metal cartons of ammunition that he assumed went with the guns.

Bill opened four more cases. One held a heavy long-rifle, this one marked .338 Lapua. The massive scope was enough to tell him that it was

212

designed for extreme long range. "Really reach out and touch someone," he said with a smile.

There were several handguns, and one case that cradled two wicked looking shotguns side by side. The weapons in these cases were all in excellent shape for having sat untouched for over a decade. For every gun there were metal flip-top boxes of ammunition that went with each. Thousands of rounds; and each ammo can had a packet of moisture absorbing desiccant.

Bill Robb danced in circles, splashing fetid water as he hooted and catcalled. "Now THIS is cake! Fuckin' cake, baby! Oh yeah, oh hell yeah!" He knew it would be days before he could wipe the huge, stupid grin off his face.

Pulling himself together he returned to the shelves, checking every container and bag. His elation continued at his fortune as he found items that would have once been considered mundane, such as razors and shaving cream, a ten-pack of disposable lighters, even a full case of cigarettes.

Once he had gone through the shelves, and his mind began to spin around a plan to get all of this treasure out and to a safer, easier to reach place he took time to sit down with one of the short PS90 guns. He spent an hour handling the weapon, oiling it from cleaning kit he had located in his search. Once the weapon was oiled and clear of any rust spots, he loaded the magazine with twenty rounds, slipped it into place and slapped it down, locking it in place on top of the rifle. "Weird, but hey, if it works, it works," he said to the corpse of Bunker Bill who was now lodged beneath the ladder.

With the gun clean, and his side-arm oiled and loaded as well, he lay back on the empty cot, resting his head on crossed arms, staring up at the concrete ceiling. "Not bad, today, Billy-boy, not bad at all. Now, if you can figure out how to get all of this shit outta here and to someplace away from the city, you'll be in grand shape. Fucking king, buddy. Fucking king."

Bill dozed fitfully, finally falling into something resembling restful sleep somewhere around 2 a.m. The then dreams came, followed by nightmares, but this day had been good, despite the tension and fear, and the nightmares quieted.

Waking early, Bill found an old military duffel and he began to fill it with supplies. The thought of humping this and his regular pack back to the car was daunting, but he was determined to carry them, no matter what. If he could move quickly he could make it back to the waiting V.W. within half a day. Carrying both bags, he expected to take most of a day.

"Time to move." He shoved six of the Meals, Ready-To-Eat into the bag, one of PS90's, (the other he would carry), one of the shotguns, a .45 from one of the plastic cases, the gun cleaning kit, and ammo for each gun. Standing below the ladder, hefting the bag, Bill swore. "Shit, I can't carry all this. Be stupid, die stupid."

He carried the bag back to the cot, sorting through it, tossing items to the side, including the second PS90, which he sealed back in its case. "I'll be back for all of it, so fuck it." Once he had the bag down to a more comfortable weight he cinched and buckled the top closed and hooked it over his shoulder.

Turning away from the cot he knocked something off the cot into the water, turning to see what it was he noticed a plastic crate sitting at the foot of the folding bed he had somehow missed.

Placing the bag back on the cot he bent over and flipped heavy latches, lifting the top of the crate. "No, fucking way!"

Nestled neatly inside the box were two rows of five canisters. Gray in color, with a series of letters and numbers, and below that the words THERMITE GRENADE followed by INCENDIARY. "Oh, damn, Bunker Bill, I don't think you're supposed to have these, buddy…"

Pawing further into the crate he found another two rows of five beneath the top layer. Twenty of the deadly canisters in all. "Oh, holy hell yeah, King, Billy, freakin' King." Carefully he placed five of the grenades in the bag, closed it up once more and climbed the ladder.

Back in the shop, Bill quickly grabbed a few small items he had set aside, like several of the bubble-packed plastic flashlights and several packs of batteries. These he shoved into the large pockets on his cargo pants.

He stood watching through the glassless barred windows for several minutes before venturing outside, through the front door. The bodies piled up outside made him work to get the door open enough to finally push the bag, then himself through.

Moving quickly, his head swiveling as if it were loose and about to fall off, Bill made for the stretch of buildings where he had left his pack. And the coffee.

He ran the two full blocks, making the very end of the row with little trouble. He wanted to get inside, gather his other gear and head out without delay.

A knot of six dead had gone unseen, loitering just inside the door of the first storefront he passed. They came out fast, and Bill reacted, not by fighting, but by ducking into the next door and bolting as fast as the heavy bag would allow for the back of the building.

Slipping on movie and CD cases, he charged through an entertainment shop that had seen better days. The dead came through the door only paces behind him, low growls preceding them.

Making for the first door he could see, Bill prayed for his luck to hold out just a bit longer. Dying in the ever-constant search for stuff was the life of a scav, and Bill knew he was good, but he wasn't ready to give up life just yet.

Bill reached out and grasped the doorknob, slowing a half step, plowing into the door. It slammed back into the wall behind it, the sound falling flat in the tiny room.

He stepped left, smashed the door close and held it for a moment, making sure the latch caught as the zombies chasing him banged into the other side.

Confident that it would hold long enough for him to reach the second floor, Bill released the knob and pounded for the stairs to his left. With the flood of adrenaline, he took the steps two at a time, hardly noticing the weight of the bag.

The landing at the top of the stairs led off to rooms along either side, just like the first apartment. Heading left again, toward the end of the building where his gear waited, Bill passed door after door, hoping to find a pass-through from one building to the next or a way up to the roof.

Just as he passed the third door, he heard a sound that tore through his ears directly into his soul, shaking him to his core. From a darkened door on the right and ten steps ahead a shape emerged.

In front of Bill Robb stood his death, and the death of all things. It was nightmare made, flesh and bone and blood. The creature was once human, though its body was contorted, misshapen now.

Its back was hunched, thin protrusions of bone lancing through the flesh along the spine. Appendages that were once arms and legs were now elongated, deformed, joints jutting awkwardly to the side as the thing moved sideways into the hall, almost crablike, and just as fast.

Bill Robb, once known as Billy Robbins to his hordes of adoring fans, cried out, terror like a barbed rod of ice spearing his heart.

Deep inside, behind the part of his mind that was seized by fear, he knew that the rumors and tall tales he had heard in his travels across the wastelands of the dead were true. The thing before him now was a Twisted, once human, it's DNA altered and body horribly changed by a virus no one living understood. He had always laughed the stories off, thinking they were a way for people to create a boogeyman worse than the zombies that roamed the world, something to displace their fear and allow them to carry on.

Bill's entire body trembled as he backed away. He shifted the bag to the other shoulder and pulled the PS90 forward on its sling, holding it one handed.

The Twisted stared at him, its huge dark eyes piercing and abrupt. The mouth opened impossibly wide and the shrieking cry came again, vibrating and reverberating inside his skull.

The creature's low-slung head dipped. Wide, split nostrils flaring, it caught a scent, Bill's scent and lifted its elongated skull. Behind him, he heard the zombies crash through the door at the bottom of the steps. Though they weren't proficient at it, they could certainly climb stairs and he was about to be boxed in.

He had no time left.

Dropping the heavy bag of supplies against the wall, he brought the weapon up and pulled the trigger. Nothing happened.

He knew his unfamiliarity with the gun was going to get him killed.

He found the safety, flicked it and spun at the sound of a groaning growl from behind him.

Runners in front and a vision of hell behind him, Bill's heart slammed a speed-metal drum solo in his chest. His throat was closing, his eyesight dimmed. He was either going to pass out or his heart would explode.

He hoped his heart would just stop. Anything was better than dying as a shared meal between death and hell.

Behind him, the creature shrieked again. In front of him, the runners stopped running. Time stuck there in that hallway as if caught on the teeth of the hounds of hell.

Not once had Bill ever seen a zombie halt its pursuit of prey.

He watched now as the runners stopped dead in their tracks. His astonishment grew when those same runners turned away. Whether in fear that he wasn't sure a zombie could feel, or simply animalistic self-preservation, they ran.

One moment he watched in shock as the dead ran away, the next he was being slammed into the wall, his head knocking a crater into the wall-board. He watched with blurry eyes as the Twisted loped after the pack on freakishly elongated limbs, catching the last in the group as they moved away down the opposite hall.

The Twisted's jaw seemed to unhinge, opening far wider than its head would appear to allow. It caught the zombie's neck in a gaping maw full of teeth and blackness and bit down, the crack of brittle bone was loud and distorted, seeming to echo within the creature's mouth. The head parted from the body with a wet snap, and the Twisted's throat swelled to impossible size as it swallowed the entire dead head whole.

The Twisted turned to face Bill, the large pitch-black eyes gazing directly into his. A shiver born of the chill coruscating through his bones ran on fleet-footed talons up his back. This thing that was once human, now a beast of agony, took one step forward with the long forelimb that had once been a left arm.

It lowered its broad head toward the matted

carpet, looking up at Bill, reminding him of a scolded dog. Its face creased and wrinkled as the mouth that seemed to be a portal to hell gaped open, bits of flesh hung from its teeth, the remains of a quick snack.

Tilting sideways, the head jerked forward several times and the mouth emitted something that sounded to Bill like a barking laugh, part hyena and part demon.

Bill stared back into the ebony depths that held him in place. The head jerked again, like a hand motioning a petulant child to be gone, followed by the bark-laugh. Then the thing blocking the hallway turned back to the fallen corpse of the zombie, pushed its face into the dead thing's abdomen and began to eat.

The snap of bone and unpleasant wet sounds filled the narrow hall, and Bill recoiled in revulsion, snapping back to himself. He bent down, snagged his bag, and backed away.

He reclaimed his voice and muttered in shock, "What in the holy dead hell…"

Sounds of the creature eating followed Bill until he found a roof access ladder and let himself out of the building. From rooftop to rooftop, he made his way toward the end of the row. He stopped for a moment to look out on the still-smoldering remains of the hair salon across the street and to assess the zombie situation street-side, before taking the crowbar from his pack and breaking open the roof access leading back into the building.

His heart was still pumping from the surreal encounter, and he used the adrenaline buzzing through his system to push himself, to gather all his gear and get out of the building as quickly as possible.

Bill retraced the route he had used to get into the suburban area, making his way back to the house from his first night in the 'burbs. Slowed by the weight of both bags and the increased zombie activity along the route it took him far longer than planned.

He had to drop his bag only once to make a kill. Coming around the corner of a peeling white house he had nearly kissed a zombie full on the mouth. If the dead could feel shock both zombie and man would have simply stared in bewilderment for a moment before realizing the situation.

But the dead felt nothing, and Bill's moment of surprise almost cost him his face. At the last second Bill jerked his head backward. He felt cold, slick lips brush the tip of his nose.

Dropping the duffel, he lunged forward, using the heavy gauntlet as a bludgeon once more, slamming it up under the zombie's chin and staggering it, giving him enough time to find his footing, draw his knife, and snap his fist forward, gouging an eye out and coring into putrid brain tissue.

Breathing heavily, he had shouldered his duffel, adjusted his backpack and carried on by using the horror and rage flooding his system to push harder.

Once he made it to the house he took stock of himself, regaining his wind and watching out the windows as dusk began to fall.

"Screw it; I'm not staying another night." A

small group of dead shuffled along the street, disappearing between two houses further down the block.

His luck held, and he made it to car in just over three hours of hard walking. His back ached miserably, and his legs felt like they were made of gelatin and hot sand. "You made it Billy, and that's all that matters," he muttered as he stowed the gear. The early darkness seemed to press in as he slid into the tiny car that reeked of the insides of dead things.

The engine chugged and huffed into life. He was only slightly dismayed to find that just one headlight worked, and the other was dim, hazy. "Can't have it all." He backed out of the trees and pointed the car in the direction of Junction.

Bill knew he was in for a long drive, and settled into the busted seat as comfortably as possible. "Eyes on the road, and if you get tired, pull over, Billy-boy." He chuckled thinking about some other scav from Junction coming along and finding him weeks or months later licking the glass, a slavering undead thing with a carload of goodies.

With the road unspooling below him and his thoughts delving into the fantasy of what a wealthy man was in the post-apocalyptic zombie world, he made the miles and hours fly by in the dark of night. The high, brilliant moon and the glitter of stars lent their light to the world, casting a strange blanket over the landscape. The lunar light covered some of the ugly, giving the dark, brutal world immediately around him a certain distorted beauty that struck a chord of sadness in his heart.

The chord reverberated, and Bill followed it

back to the land that was gone. Tender memories with jagged edges drifted up from the orchestra of his life, a soundtrack of pain and loss, love and joy that plucked with gentlest fingers at the strings of recall, stinging him.

Bill shook his head at a particularly vibrant and painful memory and focused on the road, turned his thoughts forcibly back to Junction and the elation with which others would celebrate his finds. "Oh yeah, they're gonna love it, for sure. Gonna be King and sit on my ass while others hunt down a life in the fucking rubble of yesterday," he said to the windshield, waxing poetic in his own rough way.

Landmarks he remembered well began to appear and slid by the car into darkness. "Not far to go now. Not far at all," he said.

According to the landmarks he passed he was less than ten miles from Junction when the car shuddered and rumbled when he drifted over to the edge of the road. Bill's head snapped up and his eyes popped back open just as the right wheel dropped from the pavement to the gravel and dirt along the roadside.

He yanked the steering-wheel hard, bumping back up onto the highway. Breaking slowly, Bill came to a stop in the middle of the lane, not bothering to pull over. He rested his forehead on the wheel, took a deep shuddering breath and sighed. Sleep was already pulling his eyelids closed once more. Exhaustion had finally caught up with him.

The dark lay heavy against the windows. "Screw it, I'm gonna sleep 'til dawn."

Bill knew the area here saw little in the way

of zombies wandering around, not nearly as bad as some areas, where he had seen hordes of hundreds or more roaming the countryside. Walking at night was always a risk, but carrying his heavy load, already pushing far past tired into exhaustion was asking for more trouble than it was worth.

He punched the headlight switch in, cracked the window an inch and stretched out across the two bucket seats in front. Though he was ridiculously uncomfortable, Bill fell asleep in minutes.

****

The sound of a distant gunshot yanked Bill up from his restless sleep in the space of a heartbeat. He flipped himself around into the driver's seat and slapped the pistol from its holster, braced and ready for anything.

He waited for several minutes, staring out into the dark before catching a glimpse of flickering firelight several hundred yards from his sleeping spot, off into the tall grasses and fields that ran along the side of the highway in the rural areas.

"What the hell?"

Sitting here, half asleep, Bill was fully aware that he was a fish just waiting in the barrel. "Screw this crap. Scout them out, see who they are. Not just going to wait to get my ass shot off by some nutbags who're stupid enough to go camping out in the open like that."

With his sidearm in its holster, and the PS90 slung across his neck he slipped out of the car, pushing the door closed gently. Several steps later he turned back, opened the car again and leaned into the back, rifling through the large duffel by feel alone.

The gray canisters were easy to identify, and he took four of the five he had brought with him, stuffing them into the pockets of his cargo pants.

Orienting himself to the fire, Bill ducked down into the tall grass and weeds, using the concealment nature had provided. With painfully slow movements, Bill pushed through the flora for the length of what would be almost two football fields. He stopped when he heard two voices talking quietly. Lowering himself flat in the grasses he lay down and listened.

"Everyone knows what Mitchell said. If he ain't back by tomorrow then we move on this place, tear it apart."

"I know that, assbag. What I'm asking is, does anyone have a clue what's in there? How many people, weapons, fighters? Hell, most of the towns we hit are pretty easy; people don't expect shit to go down like it does. Most let us walk right in, don't know what hit 'em until their shit is leakin' outta their heads."

"Yeah, yeah, I hear ya. I only know what little Mitchell found out. That the town has two big players, some fat-ass dude they call 'Filler' and the whore chick, uh… 'Janet', I think." They have a bunch of scavs who run through there all the time. As far as people, I don't know because he didn't know."

Bill's ears perked up at the mention of Filler and Janet's names. These bastards were talking about hitting Junction. "Uh, fuck no," he whispered into the dirt.

"One or two scavs ain't nothing, but more than that could cause us trouble, make taking it a real bitch. Those fuckers can be pretty hard, we've both seen that."

Though Bill couldn't see it, the man sitting by the fire was nodding as he chewed on something.

When the man finally spoke, Bill used the voice as noise concealment and slid forward several feet. He wanted to get close enough to see the men.

"I know, Ritchie, and we'll deal with that if it comes. We have a job to do and we're gonna do it. Find Mitchell and that damn girl. Then kill everybody in town."

Bill shook his head slowly, "Not gonna happen, dick-stick," he whispered into the dirt.

In the small silences in the conversation he could hear the soft wheezing and snores of sleep. Parting the grass in front of him he could see two men sleeping on the ground, and just beyond them the two sitting directly across from each other, looking across the small fire as they spoke.

"Dumbasses," Bill muttered with a smile. It helped knowing the two on guard duty were too stupid to know that they shouldn't be looking directly into the flames. It killed their night sight.

Bill began to circle the encampment, counting heads as he made his way around to the back side of the man who had been facing his direction. It took him over thirty minutes to make the crawling journey and his already worn and bruised body sent bolts of pain through his elbows, back and knees.

His circuit had brought him to two empty

trucks that had been beyond his sight in the dark from the other side of the fire. With his back to these he rested in the dirt and grass, considering his plan.

The two chatty, stupid, fire-gazing guards along with the ten men he had found sleeping on blankets or thin foam exercise mats meant he would have to take on twelve people. All of them fighting men.

Laying in the darkness, face in the dirt, Bill decided that either way he was going to protect Junction. The place, by many standards, was a shithole, but more than any of the other settlements he had been in, Junction was the one that he felt could be home, not just because he'd helped to start the settlement, either. In a world of shitty people, those in Junction were slightly less shitty than the rest. Except maybe for Filler.

Bill pulled all four of the incendiary grenades from his pockets and hung them by their release handles on his front pockets. He unsnapped his leg holster and checked to make sure the safety was off and a round was chambered in the PS90.

Crawling until he was less than ten feet behind the man in front of him, Bill pushed himself up into a crouch, using the man and the dark, and the night-blindness of the other across the fire to conceal him for a moment longer.

He slipped a folding knife from his pocket and carefully opened it so that it wouldn't click into place when it locked open.

With knife in hand he duck-walked closer. Walking softly between two sleepers, now three feet away from the first guard at the fire Bill stood and charged forward.

Bill slammed the knife into the back of the man's skull before the other across the fire had a chance to react to this apparition of death materializing out of the darkness.

Leaving the knife lodged in the head, Bill leapt over the falling body and the fire, which the instantly dead man fell face first into. Letting the PS90 swing free on its strap, Bill swung his gauntleted arm and connected solidly with the other man just as his cry went up into the night.

The man fell backward, out cold, but the sounds and the cut-off cry had woken several of the sleepers. More shouts went up as Bill disappeared into the tall grass and the darkness. He had not been seen.

Keeping the element of surprise, Bill yanked a grenade free and tossed it overhand into the lap of a man just now sitting up fifteen feet way. He didn't wait to see what would happen. He moved away from the position from which he thrown the first grenade. Seconds later a satisfying *whump* ripped into the previously calm night.

A brilliant glare coupled with a wild scream scored the darkness. Peering through the grass he could see all of the men on their feet, casting about for whom or what had attacked them.

Each man had a gun in hand and was fully ready to fight.

Bill snapped up the rifle, sighted in on the flat, scarred face of a man whose face seemed to shift and twitch, as if changing shape in the glare of the thermite as it burned away at the man who's screams just now stopped. "Uh-uh," Bill muttered as he fired a single round that punched through the man's nose, snapping the head pack and dropping him to the ground.

Moving again; shouts and cries of "Who the fuck's doing this?" filling the empty places in the night.

Bill popped another canister and sent it sailing into the knot of men grouped around the fallen at the fire. The grenade hit a thickly bearded man square in the face and bounced off, cracking his nose in the process.

The grenade popped, a shower of flame and heat and sparks spilling over the legs and feet of the men, sending three of them to the ground screaming.

"Six down," Bill muttered as he raised the rifle once more, popping several random shots into the camp and moving once again, back the way he had come just a moment ago.

His knees echoed the pain the men in the camp were feeling with their own special fire, the joints burning from his crouched run-and-gun.

Shots and shouts and cries filled the night along with the acrid stench of seared and burning human flesh.

Over the noises he heard someone yell out, "How fuckin' many are there damn it? I can't see a fucking thing!"

Finding the voice in the chaos, Bill sighted on another bearded man and released three shots one after the other into the chest of the questioner.

Moving to his left five feet, Bill took a knee and waited a count of thirty seconds, then he popped another canister and let it fly into the camp, continuing the frenzy.

Staying low, still crouched on complaining knees, Bill quickly made his way back around to the two trucks. Searching the bed of the first he found a plastic five-gallon gas can that felt half full when he lifted it out and moved it twenty feet away into the grass, then he unscrewed the top and prepared to fling it into the camp. The smell of fuel should have hit him right off. He dropped the container to the ground when he realized it was just water.

Back at the trucks he yanked the pin on the last canister and tossed it into the open door of the first truck. As the vehicle roared up into flame he heard someone call out, "They got the damn trucks!"

Bill chuckled as he faded back into the grass, waiting for those that would come to inspect the damage to the vehicles.

Three of the remaining five ran without caution to the burning truck. Bill dropped the first with two rounds to the chest, the second he hit in the shoulder and spun him to the ground.

The third dropped into the trampled grass next to his cursing friend. "Shitbag's hit me, damn it! Kill the assholes, man! Oh, hell, my shoulder…"

Bill calmly popped five more shots in the direction of the voice, rewarding him with a gurgling moan that quickly faded.

"Tony! Damn it, Tony!"

"Three more," Bill said softly.

Lying prone in the tall grasses, Bill watched and waited and listened. With several bodies and the truck now burning brightly shadows danced, causing

230

more confusion among the remaining three men. He kept his head low as random shots popped.

The screams of the dying and the raging shouts of the last men carried well into the cool night air. Bill knew that if it hadn't been for the darkness and his surprise attack he wouldn't have had nearly the success he did. With those elements gone taking down the last three could prove more difficult than it was worth, even if they were still disoriented and terrified.

Rising to a low crawl, Bill began the long, painful trek back to the stalled car. He could see a faint pink tint to the edge of the eastern sky. He wanted to be well down the road, hopefully at Junction's gate, when dawn rose.

Eat your heart out Bruce Willis, he thought. I could have been an action hero.

A Friend in Need is a Friend Indeed

Tool was getting worried. Frito said he was making a quick trip, but he'd been gone six days. According to Mitch Burton, Frito had headed straight east from Junction and Tool was about to do the same thing.

Normally, Tool liked to leave Junction in the middle of the night rather than midafternoon, but this was serious. He got his gear together, left Maynard with Doc and started east. It was a long shot at best. Truth was that Frito could be anywhere. Maybe he had went to his corn chip stash, only going east to throw others off the trail. Still, Tool had a bad feeling that his friend was in trouble. Friends, true friends, were a rare commodity these days and when your friend was in trouble, you did everything you could to help him.

Tool kept moving all night, slowly, looking for clues that his friend may be close by, hoping to find Frito asleep in his hammock. Around midday he saw someone moving on the road in the distance. Tool watched the figure shuffling along, moving away from him, and knew that it was not a living person. That's when he noticed blood on the pavement at his feet. A dried up puddle of blood with a tire track in it. A narrow, nearly bald tire had rolled through the blood when it was still fresh. Tool was suddenly sick to his stomach, fearing what he would have to do.

There was no mistaking that the walking corpse had once been his best friend. Tool silently removed a knife from within his jacket and thrust it into the skull with a single overhand blow. The knife sunk to the hilt. The zombie that had been Frito slumped to the ground. Tool stepped away and vomited into the grass.

After composing himself, Tool returned to the body. He retrieved his knife from the back of the zombie's skull and rolled it over to better examine it.

Frito's clothes were badly ripped and stained with blood. His camo field jacket was tattered. His prized kukri was missing as were all of his knives. The body was riddled with wounds of various sizes. Well over twenty by Tool's count. All but one had scabbed over. The one open wound oozed a pinkish slime with dark bloody streaks, the remains of a punctured lung.

Tool dragged his friend's body off the pavement and into the tall grass. After saying his goodbyes, he removed Frito's boots, tied them together and slung them over his shoulder before turning toward Junction. He cast one more glance at the gory tire-track as he walked away.

On the walk back, he formulated a plan. He would find Corey Balmont, tie him to a chair and cut little pieces off him until there was nothing left. Hopefully he could make it last for days.

Tool made it back to Junction, coming in through the North gate. He dropped Frito's boots off at his shack then went straight to Filler's, entering the back door as usual and knocking loudly on Filler's office door.

One of the girls hollered from the kitchen, "He's at the south gate, Danni came in a minute ago,

233

said that Corey kid is back."

    Tool turned and sprinted away.

To Be King in the Land of the Dead - Part 4

1

Corey stopped the rattle-trap scooter in the center of the empty highway about a mile from Junction and shut off the engine.

He sat astride the little bike, thinking. He worried that his return to Junction would not be well received after the Laidlaw incident. "Damn good thing they don't know about Frito, then," he said with a smile.

Draping his wrists over the handles, he leaned forward and peered into the distance. He could just make out the pieced-together walls of Junction in the hazy light of dawn.

"You can just turn around, find someplace else to go, you don't need this place," he said, though he knew it wasn't entirely true. Several settlements had already banned him, and he knew of one that had a bounty out on his head.

"Eh, hell, whatever happens, happens. I'll take as many of the shit-eating bastards as I can down with me if I have to."

He started the Vespa, listened to it rattle and buzz for several seconds before he slipped it into gear and finished his return to Junction.

2

Mitch Burton cocked his head and listened. Raising his binoculars, he scoped the far highway. "Well I'll be damned. That little rat-bastard is actually coming back here."

"What's that, Mitch?"

"We got a rider incoming, Danni. It's Corey. Run and get Filler." Glancing at his watch companion he said, "And hurry, I'm of a mind to just shoot this motherfucker on sight."

Danni, one of the few young women that was not in the employ of Filler or Janet, scurried down the shaky ladder and bolted for Filler's place.

The buzzing whine of the Vespa seemed to wind up tighter and more annoying as it closed the distance.

Minutes later, from behind him, on the ground Filler shouted, "Mitch, don't you shoot that boy! I want a word with him before anyone does anything, you hear?"

Danni was already climbing back up to her post.

Mitch was itching to put one of his precious bullets into the man's face as he pulled up at the gate. Shaking his head, he said, "Yeah, I got it, Filler. Don't like it, but I got it."

"Fine then. Both of you stay up there, keep an eye out, though. He pulls something stupid just drop him."

"Here's hoping," Mitch Burton mumbled.

Filler understood Mitch's anger. Though they weren't best friends, he and Laidlaw spent a lot of time together on watch. Besides, Corey could have just as easily tossed that bottle to Mitch instead of Frank.

The sound of the Vespa came to a humming idle outside the heavy gate. From outside Filler heard Corey shout up to Mitch, "Come on Mitch, open up, buddy."

"Fuck you, pisswad! I ain't your buddy. You just hold your horses." Mitch looked down at Filler and nodded.

The big man pulled the gate open slowly. He relished the wide-eyed look on Corey's face. The boy wasn't expecting him. "Idle it in here slowly, boy, and shut it down just inside the gate."

Corey nodded, keeping any snide comments to himself. He was a psychopath, but he was by no means stupid.

Filler slammed the gate shut just as Corey cut the raspy engine.

"Uh, uh, you sit right there you little fucker," Filler said with a growl when Corey began to dismount the scooter.

"Filler, listen man…"

"No, you listen kid. Frank Laidlaw may have been an ass, and he was damn sure on most everybody's shit list, but what you done was downright wrong, no matter how you twist it."

Nodding, forcing a crestfallen look onto his face during Filler's upbraiding, Corey seethed inside. To have this fat bastard facing him, chastising him like a misbehaving child was almost more than he could bear.

"I know it, Filler, and I'm sorry, I let my

emotions get the best of me, man. Really, I am.
Mitch," he said, looking up, "I'm sorry man, I know
you're pissed, I do. I can't change it, but I damn sure
won't let anything like that happen again."

The glint of disgust, of hatred in Corey's eyes
was hard to miss. "Yeah, sure, kid, I'm sure you
won't."

From inside the settlement, behind Filler a
voice called out, "Hold that little fucker!" Everyone
twitched, many pairs of eyes searching for the voice.

From between a pair of rusty, titling shacks,
strode Tool, and even from thirty feet away the look
of rage he wore was obvious.

Corey knew this was the worst time to face
off against Tool, with everyone watching. Besides,
he was sneaky, and quick. No one was sure where he
kept the little blade, but everyone knew it could pop
into being, its tip pressing into a throat or rib, in a
heartbeat. Unconsciously, Corey began to back
away.

Filler stepped up to slow Tool and thought
better of standing directly in the man's path. Like
every scav, he could be unpredictable, and Filler
knew the salvager was quick. He stood aside and held
out a wide, meaty hand.

Tool batted the hand away without slowing
and steeped toe to toe with Corey. "You did it, didn't
you, you dirty little shit-bag punk-ass *kid*? Tool
emphasized "kid", knowing full well how much
Corey hated it.

"Tool, come on, man. What are you talking
about, what did I do?"

Filler spoke up, knowing where this was

headed. "What the hell you talkin' about boy? What is it he's supposed to have done?"

Tool glanced at Filler, his eyes burning with rage. "Frito's dead," he spat. Turning back to glare into Corey's eyes, he said, "And this shit-wad is the one that did him."

To Filler's own surprise, he was shocked. Frito was just another scav, one of the many that owed him something, and like most people that made their living scavenging, Frito could be an asshole at times. A person had to be, in order to survive for any length of time outside the walls of a settlement.

Frito, on the other hand, was one of the few people that everyone seemed to like. His company was often sought out by many whenever he was in town, men for the easy camaraderie, women for the easy, well, everything else. If Filler could be said to like any scav, it was Frito.

A loud murmur passed through the growing crowd.

"Bullshit, I didn't do a damn thing to anybody! Frito, I liked him, he was a good guy, better than most of you!" For the first time in a very long time, Corey felt genuine fear.

Filler's eyes narrowed as he stared at the pasty skin, going paler even as the boy spoke. Then a high blush began to bloom on Corey's cheeks, and tears hung in his eyes.

"I was damn close to lettin' you off the Laidlaw business with a damn good ass-whippin, put you out of business for a week or so, just because you're a damn good scav, but… God damn it, kid, why Frito? What the hell did he ever do to you or

239

anybody?"

"Fuck you, Filler, you pig-fat bastard, I didn't KILL ANYBODY!"

Tools hand flicked out with precision and slapped Corey openly across his pale face. Leaning in close, nose to nose, Tool said softly, though all could hear in the silence that followed the slap, "I saw your tire tracks, Balmont. The tracks you left in FRITO'S FUCKING BLOOD!"

Corey flinched at the roar and the flying spittle; then his head was rocked back when Tool's stone-hard fist drilled into his mouth. His lips split, and he coughed, gagging as two teeth went down his throat. He crumpled to the ground.

Filler stepped up then, and Mitch clambered down from his post, both rushing to Tool's side.

"Not inside the gates, man," Mitch said. "You know the rules. Only inside the gates if there ain't another way."

Corey, dazed, his vision blurry, felt hands slip under his arms and begin to pull him along. Shaking off the haze of pain in his face, splattering his handlers with blood, he focused enough to see who they were.

Tool was on his left, Mitch was on his right, and Filler stomped the ground with heavy feet in front of him. "Guys, what are you doing?" he sputtered.

"Taking you outside the south gate, shit-head," Mitch said.

Corey screamed then, the note starting high, a scream of terror, then dropping to a low roar of rage. "Fuck you all! I'll kill every one of you backwards hillbilly assholes! I'm your fucking KING! YOUR KING, you whores!"

Bibi stood to the side, watching with her girls, who all bunched around her as the screaming murderer was dragged past, staring at them with wild eyes that caused several of them to shiver with a twinge of terror.

Filler's face was set as he led the way, a hard look that did not divert from his path. People had formed a trail behind the two dragging the third man between them, following along with all manner of weapons in hand.

Bibi turned to look at Trina standing beside her, then lightly slapped the girl's arm with the back of her hand. With a grin she said, "Best damn parade I've seen in years."

****

Bill's wrists, arms, back and knees all ached horribly, and he was relieved to see the walls of Junction loom into sight.

He was still fifty yards from the entrance when the gate suddenly opened. He was surprised, because the guards usually wouldn't open up until they had verified who was coming in. Then he saw that the gate had not opened to let him in, but to let a large group stream out, with Filler leading two men dragging a third, a procession of armed followers behind them.

Bill pulled the car in close and shut it off. He reached back in, grabbed the short rifle and slung it over his neck to hang across his chest.

He stepped toward the crowd, but hung back at the edge, watching.

He recognized both Tool and Mitch Burton dragging someone between them. It wasn't until they stood the screaming figure up in front of the deep burn pit that he knew the third person to be Corey Balmont.

"Well I'll be a son-of-a-gun. Finally caught that creepy shit at somethin'."

"I'm gonna come back and eat every one of you bastards!" the wild-eyed kid screamed.

"Huh, I somehow doubt that, boy," Bill muttered. He stepped in closer, making his way through the crowd.

"For being a piece-of-shit," Filler began, "you get a slap in the face, bitch. Tool done took care of that. For being a murderous psycho, you get dead and burned in the pit. You should feel lucky that we brain you before we throw you in and light it."

Tool stood just to the side, eyes focused beams of disgust and loathing as he stared at Corey Balmont.

Mitch held the writhing, screaming psychopath with one hand in front of the pit of charred bones and flesh that was now nothing but ash and memory. He kept a grip on his rifle, pressing the barrel into Corey's ribs.

When Filler's hand fell to the heavy pistol holstered at his side Corey's eyes widened to point that it appeared they would simply fall from their sockets to bounce on the ends of their nerve strands.

Throwing his head back and screaming to the sky, Corey twisted and shoved at the same time,

242

throwing Mitch off balance. He broke free and lunged toward Filler.

Before the heavy man could free his pistol, and with a speed that bordered on preternatural, Tool's hand snapped out, the tiny blade he kept hidden meeting with Corey Balmont's neck.

The thin, brutally sharp blade bit deep, slicing through skin and muscle, severing the murderer's esophagus before he could halt his steps.

Corey dropped to his knees in front of Filler, his hands clutching at the new gap in his neck. Blood bubbled between his fingers as he tried to speak. His mouth moved, but no words came free and he died bowing at the feet of a man he despised.

Bill rubbed absently at an imagined itch on the thick scar on his cheek while he watched Mitch spike the dead kid in the head. Tool joined him in dragging the body to the edge of the pit and tossing it in.

Pushing past several onlookers, Bill made his way to Filler.

"Seems you've had some excitement, Phil."

Watching the body as it went into the pit, Filler said, "Yeah, sure looks like it. There's always more where that came from, though." He turned to look at Bill and noticed the rifle hanging by its strap. "Spiffy new toy ya got there, Bill. Have a good run?"

"Yeah, wasn't bad at all. Had some excitement of my own on the way home. When you got a minute, I'll come sit down and tell you all about it." Gifting Filler with a huge grin that made the edges of his scar bright red he said, "I'll even make you a cup of coffee."

Filler stopped in his tracks, his head jerking around to stare at Bill. Just as he opened his mouth to speak a voice from behind them said, "Did I hear someone say coffee? Bill, did you find real coffee out there?"

Both men turned to see Bibi standing there cradling her shotgun.

Chuckling, Bill said, "Yes, ma'am, Miss Janet, I did happen to find a little. Why don't you join us, I've got a few things to tell you all anyway."

"Well, hot damn, real coffee! Lead the way, boys."

As the trio headed to Filler's, Bill asked, "So what the hell happened, anyway?"

Keeping his stride, Filler looked at Bill and Janet and smirked. "Just another day in Junction."

A New Plan

Tool wasn't happy with the day's events. He had wanted to talk to Filler about Corey, and then make a plan to catch the rotten puke, tie him up, spend days cutting little pieces off of him before finally hammering a spike into his head. Things rarely go as planned in Junction. Corey had gotten off far too easily, but it was done now and there was no way to undo it. But oh, how he would have liked to beat him to death rather than watch him bleed out at Filler's feet.

Improvise, adapt and overcome, he thought. It was time for a new plan.

The new plan was quite simple. Go to Filler's. Get something to eat. Get drunk. Get very drunk.

"Tool. Hey Tool. Stop. "

Tool was already imagining how good it would feel to lose all control. To pass out from the liquor rather than falling asleep from exhaustion.

"Tool! Hold on a minute. I want to talk to you."

Tool slowly came back to the here and now, stopping in mid stride as he realized someone was calling his name. Turning around, he saw the new gate guard, Danni, coming down the ladder.

"Tool. Got a minute to talk?"

"I guess. What's up?"

"I need your help. I want to be a scav and I was hoping you would help me."

"Are you insane? You want to go outside the walls, risk your life and end up wandering around as a zombie? Or maybe you want to be captured by Sores who will do things, terrible things, things that will make you wish you were a zombie?"

"Come on Tool. Everyone says you are the best. If you teach me, I can earn my own way around here."

"Wanna earn your own way? Go see Janet."

"Fuck you, Tool. I'm not going to work on my back."

"Knees maybe?"

"You're an asshole!" Danni turned and went back up the ladder to where Mitch was looking out over the road that lead to Junction.

Frito was dead, and Corey's body was still burning, and this girl had the guts to bring this shit up now. Tool was impressed. Guts were important, but they weren't enough. Frito had guts and he had died alone out there.

"Now back to the plan."

He stepped into Filler's and found his way to a small table in the middle of the room. As his eyes adjusted he saw Filler and Janet sitting at a table with that guy Bill. Tool couldn't recall ever seeing Filler and Janet sitting at the same table, especially not when they were actually smiling. That guy Bill seemed to hold a power over Filler. The rumor in Junction was that Filler doesn't charge him for food or anything else.

Tool signaled the kitchen girl who brought his usual bowl of thick brown stew and pitcher of water. He was just getting started on it when Mitch Burton came in.

"Mind if I join you while I wait for my to-go

order?"

Tool looked up, "Sure thing, Mitch."

"I saw you and Danni talking before. She's pretty upset that you won't help her."

Tool dropped his spoon and watched it sink out of sight.

"Tool, she wouldn't have asked for your help if there was any other option."

"Mitch, it's not like I'm the head of the scavs union. All she has to do is tell Filler she's a scav."

"She tried that. Filler shot her down."

Tool stopped staring at his stew and looked at Mitch. "Why?"

"She's going to need some stuff to get started. Filler is afraid he'll outfit her and she'll skip town without paying him back. "

"Can't blame him. It's happened before."

"Look Tool, Junction is running short on scavs and this town needs you guys. Scavs don't just bring in supplies and things to make our lives less shitty. You bring us stories and information from the outside world. You bring us a reason to keep going. Junction needs scavs."

"Mitch, I'd like to help but I'm already pretty deep in debt with Filler and with Frito gone I'm running low on friends. If I try to show her the ropes and she gets eaten by funkers I'll feel responsible."

"What if it was strictly a business arrangement? One that could help with your debt. You could work together as she learns with you keeping a share of the loot, like an apprenticeship."

"A business arrangement? It would have to lean heavily in my favor." Tool mulled it over for a few moments. "Alright, Mitch. Tell her to find me if she's serious about being a scav, but I'm telling you right now, when she dies out there I ain't takin the blame."

"Will do, Tool." Mitch grabbed his jar of stew and the bottle of water the kitchen girl had dropped off then headed back to his post.

When Danni showed up, she sat down without saying a word.

"Ok, Danni. Here's the deal. You want to be a scav. I can help, but we do it my way. I'll cover your gear with Filler, but I expect something in return."

"I told you, I'm not a whore."

"Just listen. While you're training, I keep everything we bring back. The first ten times out on your own, I get half of everything you bring in."

"NO WAY! "

"There's more. When we're inside the walls, you work for me. You do whatever I ask you to do."

"You're crazy!"

"Look, Danni, I don't really want to do this, but if I'm going to do it, I gotta get something for my efforts. Take it or leave it."

Danni was quiet for a few minutes, "The first five times out you can have half."

"Six, but we start tonight."

"Ok, but if you try any funny stuff I'll cut it off."

"We have a deal?" Tool stuck his hand out.

"Deal." Danni shook the offered hand.

"Here take this over to my shack and feed

Maynard." Tool shoved a jar of stew across the table to her. "Then come back here for your second assignment."

"What's the second assignment?"

"You're going to keep me from dying. You see, I'm gonna to drink tonight. I plan to get drunk. Very drunk. And for once, something around here is going to go exactly as I planned. Your job will be to watch me get drunk and keep me alive until morning."

Dawn's Early Light

A bright sliver of light shone through a gap in the plywood that made up the walls of Tool's little shack. As the sun moved higher in the sky the sliver of light moved across a pile of blankets to find the scav who lay unmoving on the improvised bed. When the light found his closed eyes, Tool flinched and rolled away onto the dirt floor. Maynard nosed at him as he searched for a bottle of water to wet his dry mouth and wash the hair from his tongue.

Just then, Danni entered the shack, a bottle of water in each hand. "Here. You'll be wanting to rehydrate after the night you had."

Tool took the bottle and sipped it slowly, feeling the coolness spread out from his stomach to his extremities as if his entire body was a dry sponge absorbing the liquid.

While Danni waited patiently for him to finish the bottle, she emptied the second bottle into a bowl for Maynard, stroking his side as he lapped at the water.

When she could wait no longer Danni spoke again, "When do we talk to Filler about outfitting me as a scav?"

"As soon as my head stops threatening to explode. Filler may not be real excited about our deal. I'll need to be straight if he needs some convincing."

"Speaking of convincing, what changed your mind?"

"Junction needs scavs and I need to get some debt paid. This is strictly a business arrangement, Danni. I want to get started right away so I can see a return on my investment. Is there anything you already have? Weapons? A decent pack?"

"I have a pack in my room at Trina's. One knife that I've used with reasonable success in the past."

"Alright. Filler will have everything else you need. At the very least we'll have to set you up with more weapons. Let's hope he's in a good mood. Please tell me I didn't do anything to upset the fat piece of shit while I was drinking."

"I think you're good. Filler, Janet and that new guy were having a pretty good time of their own."

"Something strange is going on with those three. Keep your ears open, Danni. And get your stuff from Trina's. You're moving in here until our deal is complete."

Danni was about to protest when Tool added, "I know! No funny business."

Danni's Deal

Tool stepped from his little shack followed closely by Danni and Maynard. The pounding in his head had settled into a dull rhythmic ache. One of the benefits of drinking on an Olympic level was the rapid recovery time.

"Take Maynard for a walk outside the gates. I'll go break the news of our deal to his greasiness, Lord Filler."

"I trust you won't be calling him that until after everything is settled?"

"I'll handle the fat man, Danni. You take care of Maynard. Don't forget, check the wall for hiding spots. Look for anyplace you could cache small items without being seen by Mitch or anyone else at the gate."

"I still don't understand why you wouldn't just turn everything in to Filler like you're supposed to."

"If you're gonna be a scav, you gotta start thinking like one. We cache a few items nearby when we have a good haul. Then when you come back empty handed you grab that stuff and turn it in."

"But if you're just going to give it to him anyway, what's the point?"

"The point is that you never want to come back empty handed. A scav that doesn't bring anything back isn't good for shit. Filler will cut you off in a second if he thinks you aren't an asset. Understand?"

"Look, I know he's a bit difficult, but surely he wouldn't."

Tool shook his head slightly then drained the last drops from the water bottle before walking away.

Danni looked down at the dog, "Come on Maynard, looks like I have homework to do."

The mutt was almost unrecognizable when compared to the filthy bag of bones who had saved Tool's life months earlier. The people of Junction seemed to like having a dog around, and the dog enjoyed the attention and the bits of food that came with being Junction's only canine.

Tool went in the front door of Filler's and threaded his way between the tables. At the kitchen counter, he shook the empty water bottle until one of the girls took notice.

From the back of the kitchen one of the girls chided him, "Hey Tool! I hear Danni is moving in with you. Must be serious. Guess you won't be coming to see me anymore."

Tool ignored the obnoxious whore and spoke to the one who brought him a fresh bottle. "Where's Filler?"

"He's out with the Beetle. Said to send you out there if we saw you."

"Really? Any idea why?"

"No. He's been pretty weird lately. Spends all his time with that Bill Robb guy. It's strange. He hasn't even yelled at any of us since that guy showed up. And all the stuff with that fat kid, Corey, we were all kinda figuring on him being more grumpy than usual."

"Ok. Thanks. I owe ya one." He turned back towards to door.

"Tool, for what it's worth, we're all sorry

about Frito."

He kept walking, not bothering to acknowledge the kind words. Everybody liked Frito, he was the nice one. Every man, woman, and child in Junction knew him and considered him a friend. The shithole of a town was a little worse without him. Hell, even this shit world, that seemingly couldn't get any worse, had somehow managed to sink a little lower.

Tool shook his head hard to clear the dark thoughts from his mind. Instantly, the thoughts were replaced by pounding pain, though it quickly receded back to the dull ache that was almost comforting. He wondered just how many more days he'd spend like this, hungover and missing his friend.

As he approached the old three-sided garage made of pallets he could see the Volkswagen. Filler had the tarp pulled back far enough to expose the motor as he poked around in the engine compartment.

Normally Tool would have gotten a bit closer before saying anything, just to piss off the fat man, but this time he decided to do the polite thing and keep a respectable distance.

"You wanted to see me?"

Filler rose to his full height and dropped a wrench into the old metal toolbox at his feet before answering.

"Tool, I know we haven't always gotten along, but I need you to do something for me. I need you to train some more scavs. I'd like for you to start with that girl Danni."

Filler paused expecting Tool to object

vehemently. Instead a wide grin spread across the scav's face.

"What's in it for me?"

"Dammit, Tool! This is important. Not just to me, to all of Junction. We need more scavs. There's some serious stuff going on and I need you to cooperate with us."

"What sort of serious stuff? And what do you mean by us?"

"I don't want to argue with you. Just take my word for it."

"Filler, I know you too well to agree to anything before I have all the facts. If you, how'd you put it, need me to cooperate, you better come clean."

Filler's face was turning red with frustration and anger. Two things that were consistently present when dealing with Tool. Worse yet, the scav was holding all the cards this time. Filler didn't like it when someone else had the upper hand, especially when it was a scav. He weighed his choices and decided against acting on his anger.

"Alright, here it is. Bill Robb went into the city. He got in and back out again without so much as a scratch, well maybe a scratch. He says that he can do it again, but there is far more than one man can carry. We want to put together a team of scavs to go in and bring out as much stuff as possible. We're not talking about canned beans here either. He found guns, ammo, the works. Enough stuff to keep Junction safe for a long time."

"How soon are you planning this little safari into Hell?"

"How soon could you have Danni up to

speed?"

"It'll be winter soon. That's a tough time to be out there. I might be able to have her ready by spring." Tool paused for effect. "Assuming I agree to teach her at all." Another longer pause, "Tell you what, since this is so important to you, I'll take her under my wing, but we do it my way. She isn't ready until I say she's ready."

"But you will make every effort to have her ready by spring?"

"Absolutely, but you'll need to get her outfitted. Some knives, a decent pack, blankets, the works."

"That's shouldn't be a problem." Filler was smiling now. He couldn't help but feel that he had won a small victory.

"Oh, and you'll need to pick up the tab for that stuff. I don't want her going into this with all that debt hanging over her head, might slow down the learning process."

That feeling of victory began to slip away, replaced once again by anger and frustration. "Wait just a minute! You can't expect me to carry her!"

"I'm the one training her. I'm the one who'll be out there with her. You want me to do this, we do it my way! Do we have a deal or not?"

Filler's face was flushed. His hands were clenched into tight fists that shook with the strain. This was not how he had pictured this conversation ending.

"Fine." Filler seemed to deflate as he relaxed his hand and extended it the scav. "We have a deal."

The two men sealed their agreement with a

handshake before Filler asked, "Are you going to talk to her, let her know?"

"Sure. I'll get her on board then send her over to get some gear."

"Any idea where she is? I haven't seen her today. Usually she takes Mitch his breakfast."

"Filler, you really need to pay better attention to the goings on in our little community."

The scav walked away without further explanation. As the big man pulled the tarp back over the old Beetle he had the nagging feeling that he was missing something.

END

Bites and Scraps

Let me preface the following snippets of life in and around Junction by saying that these are posts originally from the Tales of Junction Facebook page. There is no rhyme and little reason to these. Consider them an added glimpse into the lives of those people doing all they can to survive in Junction. There's no order, and they do not impact the overall tale in any meaningful way. Enjoy.

***

If you think life is tough now, just wait til you get to Junction.

***

Welcome to Junction

A place where those who scavenge are rock stars, the doctor is a drunk, and prostitutes double as teachers and waitresses.

***

Welcome to Junction.

If you've made it this far, you either have serious survival skills or you have been damn lucky.

***

"You wanna make me out to be a villain, I'm okay with that. Hell, I'm good at it. But keep in mind that it's just temporary. At some point all of Junction will know the truth. They'll all know who started this shit and they'll all know who the real villain was."

Tool

***

Bixsey liked to watch. It was one of the very few things he was good at, watching. He preferred to be tucked away somewhere quiet, away from the eyes of others.

Bixsey hated being watched.

He watched now, from a safe distance. He watched the people sitting high on their lookouts behind the walls. He watched as people went in and out of the gates, though it didn't happen too often.

He didn't know names, and could barely see faces, even when looking through the broken rifle scope, so he gave people names based on what he could see.

There was Fat Pig, who he'd watched feed the small drift of pigs. There was the one who looked like a washed-up rock star that he called Junkie Rocker. There was another that he'd once seen toss what had looked like a little snack chip package. He called him Tater Chip. Tater Chip was often seen with Junkie Rocker.

Propping himself higher on his elbows, Bixsey raised the glass, looking at the man he called Eyeball standing on a lookout post behind the wall.

Bixsey smiled when he saw the man raise his rifle, thinking there might be some action, then he realized that Eyeball was pointing the rifle in his direction.

He didn't hear the shot or feel the bullet that grazed his temple and put him out like a switch had been thrown.

***

When it rains...

Rain is a wonderful thing in Junction. Everyone stands out in it, enjoying the feel and smell. Many openly bathe in the streams running off the tin roofs of their little shacks.

Filler has his girls arrange barrels to catch as much as possible to use in the gardens and for the hogs.

Even old Doc Shoup will move his chair outside, sit on his porch dozing with a bottle in his lap.

The best part of the rain, in Tool's opinion, is that for at least a short time the smell of junction is washed away. The smell of unwashed bodies, poor sewage, and those damn pigs disappears, even if only for a few hours.

***

As Frito searched the old farm house looking for small treasures, anything that might be useful to the citizens of Junction, his mind began to wander. His high school history class came to mind. He could still recall the face of his teacher, Mr. Harshbarger, and the ridiculous tie the man often wore, a huge outdated thing with paisley print. In his mind he heard the man droning on about the gold rush and how the men dug or panned for gold in hopes of finding the mother lode that would buy them a life of leisure. Day after day these men worked hard, risking their lives in the cold and rain, never sure if they would be killed by a claim jumper, an outlaw, indians or the elements. It must have been a horrible existence.

***

This could be one of the Twisted. Can't nobody really know for sure. Every person that's lived to talk about 'em sounded stark raving mad so the stories become rumor, myth. Folks in Junction sure do love their stories too. The best stories are the true-ta-life ones with just a little somethin' extra added for kick.

Sometimes I think about the way things were. How easy life was. Even when it seemed hard, it was easy compared to now.

Mostly I think about the movies we watched. The zombie flicks were my favorite. They seemed so real and so far out at the same time. Now that I'm living in one, it's the mistakes that mostly come to mind. The things the movies got wrong.

In the movies, they always talk about how bad the undead smell. They got that part right, but nobody ever mentioned how bad the living smell. We all live like animals now. Water is far too precious to waste on bathing or washing clothes. The best we can do is pray for rain, stand outside and try to wash off some of the stench. It never goes completely away, but you have to try. I've seen the old boarded up schools where groups of people live together. It must be horrible inside. All those unwashed bodies sharing the same space. Most days my own smell bothers me, I can't imagine what it's like to be under the same roof with dozens of stinking people.

The other thing the movies got wrong was the flies. Flies don't bother zombies. Normally flies are attracted to rotting meat of any species, but they seem to sense that the infected are somehow tainted. In fact, all the animals leave them alone. Birds don't pick at them like in the movies. Even after a zombie is "killed" the animals avoid it. Nobody wants to be around them, regardless of their status as undead, dead, or other. Guess it is fitting.

For the record, zombies don't moan. Or maybe I should say they can't moan. In order to moan or scream or talk, animals force air over their vocal cords. Since zombies don't breathe, they can't moan. It seems like a small thing, but for those of us trying to survive in a world teeming with undead, it really is a big deal.

While we're on the subject, zombies don't shuffle either. Romero was way off with this one. Don't get me wrong, they aren't going to win any races, but they are not the shambling uncoordinated corpses the early movies made them out to be. If you just keep moving, you can easily outdistance one, assuming you have room to run. The problem is, you have to rest eventually while they do not.

The eyes are wrong in the movies too. I was careless once and ended up nose to nose with one. As you might imagine it was not a pleasant experience. After staring into its eyes for what seemed like hours, there was obviously something weird about them. They weren't cloudy or milky like Hollywood made them out to be. Have you ever seen a puddle of water with hundreds of little tadpoles swimming in it? That's how their eyes looked. You could actually see small things swirling around just below the surface. It was unnerving to say the least.

Unnerving. That's a serious word to be throwing around in this world.

***

A scav came through today and kind of threw everyone off a bit. He sat down in Filler's and had some of the brown stew, chatting up a storm, telling everyone about a group of sores he'd run across a week previous. Then he said something that seemed to quiet everyone down for a minute. He'd looked at an old calendar, and figured up the days. Today was July the 4th, America's Independence Day.

It was odd to think about. One of those things that people had forgotten about over the years. Most of the younger ones had no clue.

But some, guys like Filler and Bill Robb, who had been in town for about two days this trip, and Doc Shoup, they got all quiet and maudlin. I know I was feeling it myself. Yeah, I know, Bibi Reno, getting all emotional over some long-forgotten holiday, but damn if it didn't make me feel a tad heart-sick, thinking about it.

***

So many things happening, most of them freakin' scary as hell, even for Junction. I'm pretty sure I saw someone skulking around outside the west wall today when I was dumping off some gray-water from the kitchen.

Filler just ignored it, told me I was seeing things and to get my "skinny ass back to work."

He never seems to complain about it being skinny on the rare occasion when he gets his.

I'll be keeping my eye open. Besides, that Balmont kid could show up at any time. He scares me, and most of the girls, though we wouldn't tell anyone that.

***

No one gives a shit. Not what you look like, not what your personal preferences are. The only thing that matters is what you can bring to the survival of Junction and its people.

The scavs know this. The whores know it. Janet and Filler know it.

The survival of Junction and its people. That's what matters.

***

Full Moon Celebration

Every full moon was a celebration. For two days, we would gather firewood. The children gladly helped, knowing that Full Moon meant staying up late, listening to music and stories, then falling asleep in their mother's arms. Everyone sang along to the songs but as the fire burned low the story tellers took over. The village would grow quiet as the elder men took turns recounting events of their lives and of their ancestors. Tales of hunting the large brown bears or giant stag. Stories of war, battles between the clans of old. We knew all the stories as well as we knew the songs. They were the same each celebration, yet each time was as chilling as the first telling.

But even now, after all these years, there is one story that means the most to me. I guess we all have our favorites. Most of the men favored hunting stories. The adolescent boys were enthralled with stories of heroic warriors. My favorite was told by Grandmother.

She was the oldest woman in the village. Very little of consequence happened without her approval. Hunting, planting, the harvest, all these things were left undone until she gave a nod.

I was in my twelfth year before I ever heard her tell the story. She told it only a few times during my life, but every word has remained with me. It is not mine to share and I could not do it properly under any circumstances so I will not recount it here. Suffice to say that it was a true story, pure and unembellished. Unlike the exaggerated hunts, hers required no creative liberties, no artistic license. Hers was a true story of love.

It was an impossible love. Not the easy kind found in our village, where the children play and grow up together, eventually pairing and having children of their own. No, the story Grandmother told was about the best kind of love. The kind that defies all the odds. The kind of love that few will ever experience and fewer still can endure.

Being young and not knowing any better, one day, I asked her if it was true. Her eyes, usually solemn and still, began to sparkle as she looked down at me and nodded. "Is it your story? Did it happen to you?" Again, she nodded. Her eyes began to dance as a smile creased her weathered face. She placed a hand on my shoulder. Whether out of tenderness or simply to steady herself, I do not know, but it seemed she swayed a little as if her knees were going weak. She glanced away then, turning her face into the autumn breeze she repeated the last line of her story, "He had such pretty eyes."

***

Everything from the old world was valuable to the residents of Junction. Problem is, not much of the old world survived.

***

Months after the grid went down for good I was sitting at home relaxing when it hit me. What about those poor bastards with their electronic books? iPads and Kindles and all that stuff. In a moment of panic I glanced across the room to rows of books lining the wall. Shelf after shelf filled with everything from westerns to sci-fi. Wood working to metal forging. I'd accumulated quite a library over my fifty odd years but what about those poor e-book people? What were they doing? How did they spend the long afternoons? How did they refresh their memories on subjects like bee keeping or grafting fruit trees? For a moment I felt pity, but the feel of warm paper in my hand comforted me, beckoned me to return to its pages. Fahrenheit 451 has always been a favorite of mine.

***

The girls in Filler's employ all agreed that he was not the worst boss in the world. Mostly because they had all experienced life outside the walls of Junction. They had scars from hiding in the trunks of burned out cars, nightmares from the men who had locked them in old tractor trailers or beat them into submission. As long as they worked for Filler the girls were under his protection. He was a powerful man in Junction, nobody dared treat them badly. Each of them had a small room that locked from the inside, plenty of food and water, and of course they got to bathe regularly.

Bathing was a bit of a luxury in Junction, but Filler insisted the girls keep themselves clean. Not because they were required to work in the kitchen, there were no health inspections these days. His motivation was purely a matter of marketing. Clean girls attracted more customers.

The ones who were not actively working in the "back rooms" still had plenty to keep them busy.

There was gardening, cleaning and operating the stills, caring for the hogs, preparing and cooking meals. The days were full and chores were carried out according to a schedule that Filler posted weekly.

Most of the inhabitants of Junction assumed that Filler was taking liberties with his employees. This simply was not true. On the rare occasions when Filler had an urge, he treated it as a standard transaction and noted it as such in the books. The girl received credit for her "work" just as she would with any other customer.

Occasionally one of his employees would decide to strike out on her own. If she was not deep in debt, Filler would typically bid her a fond farewell. As there was not much work for a woman in Junction, after a few weeks most willingly returned, preferring the security of Filler's establishment to the uncertainty of daily life in an uncaring world. A few joined up with pilgrim groups passing through Junction on their way to some fairytale community and were never seen again.

***

Tool, Junction is running short on scavs... Scavs don't just bring in supplies and things to make our lives less shitty. They bring us stories of the outside world. They bring us a reason to keep living. In short, Junction needs scavs.

***

The funkers were nasty. All zombies sucked, but she hated funkers more than any of the other mutations. The skin that appeared to be melting, dripping from the body in wattles and tatters that would flap wetly in a stiff breeze. The exposed

266

muscle tissue, decomposing on the walking corpses, had a greenish cast to it when seen in the full light of day.

Emmalee watched as the group of three funkers dragged their feet in the dry grass, leaving a trail behind them, bits and pieces of stinking gore clinging to the grass or mixing with the dirt to create a foul mud.

She waited until they were well past the snarl of wrecked vehicles she hid in before she thought about running. Junction was still miles away, and she hoped to make it before nightfall.

Standing tall, she gripped the worn pack in her right hand and a rust-dulled hatchet in the other. She peeked around the back of an overturned bus, ensuring that the funkers were well on their way when she heard a shriek.

Emmalee turned as the runner dived over a burned-out Buick. There was no backing away, nowhere to run to. The zombie's mouth met hers in deadly a make-out session, its nose pressing against her cheek as its top teeth pushed into her mouth. Screaming was impossible now. The runner clamped its lower jaw tightly and jerked, yanking her back and forth.

Tears spilled from her eyes as her own jaw began to separate, the tendons and tissue ripping under the vicious onslaught. Darkness closed in on her vision, and she welcomed it, letting the pain take her to the dark place just as the sound of chewing filled her ears.

***

Junction. It isn't much to look at. Little more

than a collection of burned out vehicles and rickety buildings inhabited by some of the worst that humanity has ever offered up. To be honest, there isn't much humanity left. Those of us who survive in this place do whatever it takes to get by. It is rarely pleasant, but few things are in our world.

Life inside the walls of Junction is safe only by comparison. Outside is a wasteland inhabited predominantly by the undead. The few people who live out there do so only because they aren't welcome in our little community of scoundrels and whores. We call them "Sores." It's difficult to tell which is more dangerous, the Sores or the zombies.

The Sores are at least somewhat predictable. The zombies, however, seem to be in a constant state of change. The virus that created them continues to mutate, making it impossible for us to know ....

END

About the Authors

John L. Davis IV- I write things. I've been doing it for a really long time, but only recently did I start publishing. Soon after that I was lucky enough to land a job as the editorial assistant for a small newspaper. Now someone actually pays me to write, which is pretty cool. Other than that, I have no credentials to speak of, no education worth noting. I haven't done anything amazing like single-handedly save an entire tribe of Ugandan children from Ebola or serve overseas and save my entire squad from a tribe of Ugandan children with Ebola.

Along with the indie self-published American Revenant zombie apocalypse series set in and around Hannibal, Missouri I dabble in horror and science-fiction, mostly in short stories. I've also written several short screenplays with plans to eventually script a feature-length film.

If you need more zombie survival horror, read the American Revenant series today!

Guy Cain - I can't remember a time when I wasn't enjoying the outdoors. As a child my father taught me to hunt and fish. Later, in the Boy Scouts, I found that the nature merit badges were my favorites to earn on my trail to Eagle Scout. Years after, it occurred to me that the things I had learned in my youth were not common knowledge. In fact, many simply had no clue how to behave in the outdoors, let alone survive in it. Ultimately, I founded Zombie Apocalypse Survival Camp to help families learn together so they can perform as a cohesive unit in the event of a catastrophe.

Somewhere along the way I tried my hand at writing articles on some of the less obvious aspects of survival, like possible apocalypse currencies, using brush piles for survival, and more. A few of these have been published in Backwoodsmen Magazine.

Whether it's hunting, fishing, camping or just a nice long hike with my dogs, for me, being outdoors is the remedy to all life's problems.

Read more great stories from Guy Cain, available at Amazon.com!

If you enjoyed the Bites and Scraps section, follow the Tales of Junction Facebook page.

We are working with a fellow apocalyptic author, actor, and filmmaker to bring you the best of all things Post-Apocalyptic. Visit ApocalypseGuys.com to find out more.

Made in the USA
Columbia, SC
08 February 2025

52884239R10152